"Do you want me to go?" he asked her.

"You probably should." The words came out in a whisper.

"But I asked if you wanted me to."

He held her gaze. "No," she said. "I don't want you to leave."

He exerted pressure on the back of her neck until her lips hovered within inches of his. "Kiss me good night, Piper."

She couldn't. She could only stare mutely and wonder where her good sense had fled to.

"Then I'll have to kiss you," he said. His lips pressed against hers and his tongue slid inside her mouth, parting her lips with a gentle pressure. She tasted temptation, exquisite temptation, a temptation that washed away her fears in an explosion of feeling. Helpless, her tongue met his in an erotic dance of pure pleasure while his hands fell to the lapels of her robe, hesitating a moment before he parted the material and touched her breasts.

"Eric," she said in a strangled whisper.

"Shh." He raised a hand to bring her mouth back down to meld with his, kissing her deeply, a slow, sweet dizzying torture of the senses.

"Eric, this isn't—we can't—"

He drew the lapels of her robe together over her chest, pulling her closer. His hands rested lightly at the valley of her breasts; their lips were a scant inch apart. "You're kidding yourself, you know."

WHAT ARE *LOVESWEPT* ROMANCES?

They are stories of true romance and touching emotion. We believe those two very important ingredients are constants in our highly sensual and very believable stories in the LOVE-SWEPT line. Our goal is to give you, the reader, stories of consistently high quality that may sometimes make you laugh, sometimes make you cry, but are always fresh and creative and contain many delightful surprises within their pages.

Most romance fans read an enormous number of books. Those they truly love, they keep. Others may be traded with friends and soon forgotten. We hope that each LOVESWEPT romance will be a treasure—a "keeper." We will always try to publish

LOVE STORIES YOU'LL NEVER FORGET BY AUTHORS YOU'LL ALWAYS REMEMBER

The Editors

Loveswept ® 837

MIDNIGHT REMEDY

EVE GADDY

BANTAM BOOKS
NEW YORK · TORONTO · LONDON · SYDNEY · AUCKLAND

MIDNIGHT REMEDY

A Bantam Book / May 1997

ISBN 0-553-44580-4

Published simultaneously in the United States and Canada

*Bantam Books are published by Bantam Books, a division of Bantam
Doubleday Dell Publishing Group, Inc. Its trademark, consisting of the
words "Bantam Books" and the portrayal of a rooster, is Registered in
U.S. Patent and Trademark Office and in other countries. Marca Regis-
trada. Bantam Books, 1540 Broadway, New York, New York 10036.*

PRINTED IN THE UNITED STATES OF AMERICA

OPM   10 9 8 7 6 5 4 3 2 1

This is for Kathy Wilson, who started me down the road, and for Jean Price and Dee Pace, who are always there for me.

And for Bob, Diana, and Chris, who give me love, joy, and inspiration.

ONE

"Dammit, Gus, do you *try* to hit every blasted pothole on the road?" Eric Chambers glared at the old man as the battered pickup bottomed out with yet another bone-rattling, gut-busting thud.

"Eh? What's that?" Gus cupped a hand to his ear and flashed him a yellowed grin.

After Eric's car had died on the deserted west Texas road and he began walking in the hundred-plus-degree heat, the wizened old man in the beat-up pickup had seemed like a godsend. Some godsend. Eric had managed to hitch a ride with the Good Samaritan driver from hell.

"Funny thing, you wantin' to go jest where I was headed," Gus said, cackling.

Grunting in answer, Eric shut his eyes, blocking out both the sight of Gus's shaggy head and the mountain road boasting shoulders that dropped off into nowhere and potholes the size of Lake Texoma. Funny thing they were going to the same place, was it? In this uninhabited part of the state odds were any car he saw would be going where he was.

Piper Stevenson would have a lot to answer for when he finally came face to face with her. *She* was the reason he was stuck in an ancient pickup with a man so old he made dirt look young. *She* was the reason he'd had to take time off from his practice to talk about a claim that couldn't possibly hold water. And *she* was the person who'd convinced his patient that she'd cured him with her blasted herbal medication. God only knew what she'd put in that herbal tea she'd given Randy Johnson.

Eric intended to find out, and he also intended to tell Ms. Piper Stevenson to keep her herb-pickin' hands off his patients.

The pickup shuddered to a halt outside a one-story ranch-style house badly in need of fresh paint. Plants bloomed profusely and a dogwood tree flowered in the front yard.

"Any ideas where Ms. Stevenson might be?" he asked Gus.

"In there," the old man said, jerking his head at a long L-shaped building of green painted wood and glass panes. A greenhouse, obviously. A couple of windows were cranked wide, opened to the outside.

"Thanks for the ride," Eric said, at the same time thanking God he'd reached the place alive. His con-frontational mood reinforced by the horrendous ride, he strode to the greenhouse. A huge dog lay stretched across the threshold, snoring loudly. Eric halted, won-dering if he should try to shift the animal or try to step over it, but it raised its head and gave a sleepy woof. Then it thumped its tail and rose, stretching long and languidly before ambling away. Unaccountably annoyed even more—and by a dog, for Pete's sake—Eric grabbed the door handle then paused, remembering the advice Dave Burson, his former colleague, had given him.

"Don't tick her off until you've found out for sure if it's bull or not," Dave had said. "Think of it, Eric, a cure for—"

"Right," Eric had interrupted. "She's got a cure like I'm going to be the next Surgeon General. Give me a break. You don't believe it any more than I do."

"Hey, it's a possibility you can't afford to ignore. It's one I can't afford to ignore, anyway. What if it is a cure? It worked for the Johnsons."

Dave was right, dammit. *Something* had worked for the Johnsons, and he was going to have to at least be civil to Ms. Stevenson until he found out more. But once he had proved that Randy Johnson's cure had only been coincidental to his drinking that herbal tea, he'd blast Ms. Stevenson's ears with what he thought about practicing medicine without a license.

He jerked open the door and stopped in midstride. Stunned, he absorbed the fantasyland of colors and smells, an oasis set in the midst of a spartan west Texas ranch. The long, narrow room exploded into vibrant hues and confusion, crammed full with plants in every stage of growth and every color of bloom. Though there was probably some order to the greenhouse, Eric's immediate impression was one of wild disarray. The scents of damp earth and blossoming flowers gave the humid atmosphere a tropical flavor, which blended well with the exotic flair of the plants.

He didn't see a sign of human inhabitants until he

made his way into the next section of the greenhouse. If possible, it held even more flowers and other assorted greenery, including what looked to Eric like weeds. His quarry stood in a corner of the cramped room, surrounded by plant cuttings, clay pots, and dirt.

"Where in blazes have you been, Gus?" she asked without turning around. "We've got to get the orchids sprayed today."

"Ms. Stevenson?"

She turned to look at him. Her eyebrows lifted in a faint question. "Yes. Can I help you?"

Blond, curvy, pretty—No, he thought, pretty didn't cover it. In her own way, she was as much of a contradiction as the flowers. What was a knockout whose sweet-hot drawl hit him like Southern Comfort on an empty belly doing digging up dirt in a greenhouse in the middle of nowhere? Business, Eric reminded himself, realizing he stared. You're here on business. "Eric Chambers," he said, offering his hand.

She started to offer hers, but drew it back before he touched it. "Sorry. Mud," she said by way of explanation.

"Dr. Chambers," he repeated, dropping his hand. "From Capistrano. We had an appointment."

"Appointment?" Her brow furrowed. "To see the plants? I'm afraid I don't—"

"No, not the plants. It's about the Johnsons."

"The Johnsons?"

Why did she look so mystified? "Randy and Virginia Johnson. Friends of yours, I understand?"

"Yes, but I really don't see—"

"I made the appointment yesterday. With your husband, perhaps?"

"Oh, I doubt that," she said, her smile tight, "since I'm not married."

"Whoever he was, he said he'd tell you. I take it he didn't."

"You take it right. But you probably talked to my grandfather, so I'm not surprised. He forgets stuff like that all the time."

"Typical," Eric muttered, beginning to feel impatient. "Well, since I'm here could we discuss this matter? I'm on a tight schedule and I'm not sure I can get back this week."

Her sky-blue eyes assessed him critically, as if he were a plant she suspected of having aphids or some other undesirable quality. Though she still looked confused, she finally said, "All right. We might as well go to the house."

They retraced his previous path through the building, only this time the woman in front of him distracted Eric even more than the plants had. As they stepped outside, a small boy catapulted from the back door of the nearby house and ran straight at them. Reaching Piper, he clutched her around both legs.

"It wasn't my fault, Mom," he said, looking up at her.

"What wasn't your fault?"

"I was just tryin' to feed it."

"You murdered your crab." She seemed unsurprised.

"Didn't murder it," the child said sulkily. "He wouldn't come out."

"Didn't I tell you if you pulled that hermit crab out

of his shell, you'd kill it?" Exasperation colored her voice.

"Just dropped him a *little*, Mom, honest."

"From where, the top of the refrigerator?"

The child hung his head and started crying. Piper smoothed a hand over his blond hair and said, "Never mind. We'll discuss this later. Where's Grandpa?"

"Dunno." The tears dried like magic. "Jason wants me to come to his house and play. Can I?"

"If it's all right with his mom." Before he could disappear, Piper added, "Cole, this is Dr. Chambers. My son, Cole."

"Hi," Eric said, thinking that the kid looked like a small clone of his mother.

"Hi. Are you an animal doctor?" Cole asked. Hope brightened his eyes.

"Sorry, sport. Just people." It didn't sound like there was much chance for the crab anyway, from what he'd heard.

"Oh. You didn't come to see Grandpa, did you?"

"No, I came to see your mother."

"That's good, 'cause Grandpa don't like people doctors. Yesterday I heard him say that if that sorry son of—"

"Cole! How many times do I have to tell you not to repeat what Grandpa says to Sam?"

Cole grinned impudently. "Oh, yeah, I forgot. 'Bye," he said to Eric, and ran off.

"Poor Herman," Piper said, shaking her head. "He lasted longer than I thought he would, though. I gave him a week, tops, and it's been two."

From what little he'd seen of the kid, Eric was surprised the crab had lasted a day. Wisely, he didn't make that observation aloud.

Piper led the way into the house through the back door. Once inside the kitchen, she turned to her unexpected visitor. "So, I guess you're the new doctor from Capistrano?" What in the world did he want with her and what did it have to do with Randy and Virginia Johnson? Piper supposed she ought to give him a chance to explain, especially after Cole had all but insulted his profession. He'd taken it in stride, though. She could have sworn she'd even seen a smile hovering around the corners of his mouth.

"That's right," he answered. "Let's talk aphrodisiacs, Ms. Stevenson."

"Let's not," she said. Great, was the new doctor a quack?

"Herbal tea, then." He gestured impatiently. "Whatever you want to call that concoction you gave Randy Johnson."

This was getting weirder by the minute, Piper thought. Concoction? "Excuse me? What the devil are you talking about?"

His eyes narrowed. "I want to know why you were treating my patient. *My* patient, Ms. Stevenson, not yours. Just what kind of aphrodisiac were you giving him in that herbal tea?"

Arrogant jerk, she thought, shooting him a withering look. "Herbal tea? Aphrodisiacs? You're a little confused, Doctor. I don't treat people. I sell them plants."

"You must have forgotten that when you decided to treat Randy Johnson."

It was really too bad, she thought, her gaze sweeping

over him from top to bottom, that he was so cute. And that he had such gorgeous green eyes. If there was any justice at all, his looks would match his overbearing personality. "Are you sure the Johnsons are your patients?" she asked, eyeing him distrustfully.

He ground his teeth. "Of course I'm sure. Don't be absurd. Randy and Virginia Johnson sent me to you. Call them if you feel the need to check my credentials."

She mulled that over, irritated at him, yet curious about his reasons for being there. Herbal tea, aphrodisiacs, and the Johnsons. Where was the connection? There was one way to find out. "Okay, we'll talk," she said, motioning to a chair at the kitchen table.

Frowning, he took a seat.

Piper grabbed a faded blue plastic pitcher from the refrigerator. "Want some?"

He eyed the pitcher dubiously. "No, thanks."

"It's not herbal tea. Good old Lipton's, FDA approved."

His lips quirked. "In that case, yes, please." As she reached for the glasses he added, "You've got a smart mouth, Ms. Stevenson."

"Self-defense." She threw him a pointed look over her shoulder. "It comes from years of people assuming blond equals dumb."

"You left out beautiful." His gaze slid down the length of her back before returning to meet her eyes.

Her breath caught at the unexpected comment. "Why, Dr. Chambers, a compliment?" she asked sweetly. "I'm flattered."

"Don't be. I merely stated the obvious."

Obvious? Jerk, she thought again, slamming his glass

of iced tea down so hard, tea sloshed out onto the table and dribbled off the edge onto his slacks. Reacting instinctively, she grabbed a dish towel and tried to blot up the tea. For an eternal, electrically charged moment, she froze with her hand on his thigh—high on his thigh. Her face flushed, and she snatched her hand away and jumped back, throwing the dish towel toward the drainboard as if it had bitten her.

"Thank you," he said solemnly.

Their gazes met and he smiled. She wanted to sink into the floor from sheer embarrassment.

"Now, are you going to tell me what was in that concoction you gave the Johnsons?"

"The only thing I ever gave Virginia was a dry-skin remedy. She bought the herbs from me to make it up at home."

"Dry-skin remedy? She told me you gave her an aphrodisiac."

"Well, I didn't." Crossing her arms over her chest, Piper leaned back against the counter. "Herbal mixtures are a hobby of mine, but the things I make are cosmetic, not therapeutic."

"Virginia and Randy Johnson say the recipe you gave them cured him."

"Cured him of what, for heaven's sake?"

"Impotence."

For a moment, she could only stare at him. Then she burst out laughing. "*Impotence?* Oh, Lord, that's the best joke I've heard in a week. I promise you, if Virginia got an aphrodisiac, she didn't get it from me. The herbs I gave her were for dry skin."

Unamused, Dr. Chambers went on. "Virginia Johnson is pregnant now and she claims that your remedy is the reason why."

"That's ridiculous."

He inclined his head in agreement. "That's what I thought too."

"Oh, really? If you thought it was such a crock, then why are you here?"

"Because Randy Johnson is my patient," he said irritably. "Even though I don't believe your herbal mixture had a blessed thing to do with Mr. Johnson's cure, they believe it. They are so firmly convinced that your remedy works, and so insistent on continuing to use it, they've given me permission to discuss their case with you. You can appreciate how difficult that was for them. Now I want to know what's in that remedy. I intend to make certain that this stuff won't harm Randy."

"How could it? It's not for ingesting. It's to rub on your skin."

"I knew it," he said, shaking his head, a look of disgust on his face. "That's what's wrong with you people dabbling in things like this. Randy Johnson drank that remedy."

"Drank it?" Piper asked, her mouth dropping open. "Good God, you're not supposed to drink that. It might have made him sick."

"Exactly," he said dryly. "But they didn't ask me, they just told me after he'd done it. He thought it was herbal tea and he liked it so much he drank it several times. Two months later, Mrs. Johnson turns up pregnant."

"And you think my recipe did the trick."

"No. The Johnsons think that. I think—" He broke

off in midsentence. "I think that medications should be prescribed by an M.D. We're talking practicing medicine without a license, Ms. Stevenson."

Jamming her hands on her hips, she faced him defiantly. "Don't try to scare me, Dr. Chambers. Those herbs weren't even meant for Randy."

"But the fact remains that he took them."

"It's not my fault he drank the stuff. I told Virginia exactly what to do with it." Hadn't she?

"Did you?"

Lord, he was sharp. He'd instantly picked up on her momentary qualm. "I can't believe it would help him, anyway. There wasn't anything purported to be an aphrodisiac in that mixture." She frowned in concentration and tapped her fingers on her arm. Doubtfully, she added, "At least, I don't think there was."

"Don't you know what you gave her?" He raised his eyebrows.

"Of course I do, it's just—" She stopped and looked at him suspiciously. "Now wait just a minute. Are you trying to trick me into giving you the ingredients?"

"Why? Is it a secret formula or something?" Regarding her with more than a hint of condescension, he sipped his tea. "Come now, Ms. Stevenson, you said yourself it's merely a dry-skin remedy. Aren't you being a little ridiculous?"

Ridiculous, was she? She'd had just about enough from him. Placing her hands on her hips again, she faced him loaded for bear.

"Aren't you being a little offensive? No, let me rephrase that. You're being extremely offensive. You attacked me from the moment you stepped into my greenhouse. *My* greenhouse, Doctor. Let's see." She held up a hand and started ticking items off on her fingers. "First I stole your patient. Next I'm practicing medicine without a license. Before I know it, you'll be accusing me of drug trafficking. Tell me, Dr. Chambers, why in the heck should I tell you a thing about my herbal mixture?"

For a long moment he stared at her, then a smile spread over his face. "I didn't mean to be offensive. My concern for my patient made me overreact."

Tricky devil, she thought, but she was a bit mollified, nonetheless. When he smiled he didn't look arrogant. He looked almost . . . sweet, but with a bit of the devil thrown in too. Women probably ate up that clean-cut charm.

"You still haven't given me a good reason to tell you," she reminded him.

"Look, if there's a chance that your remedy might help people with this problem, don't you think we ought to pursue it?"

"No." He didn't really believe it would help. Hadn't he just said so? And she didn't think so, either.

"No?" He stared at her as if the word were totally beyond his comprehension. Then his expression slowly changed to one of puzzlement and . . . alarm? He looked down at his thigh and plucked something off it. "What the—"

"Herman!" Piper exclaimed. The little creature he held was about two inches long, mostly thin legs and eyes, staring at them from the safety of its shell.

"The late Herman, I take it?" His lips twitched as he placed the hermit crab in her outstretched hand.

"Oh, Cole will be so glad." Happily, she stroked a finger over the shell. "Thank you." He was staring at her as if he seriously doubted her sanity. "What?" she asked.

"Nothing. I've just never gone into someone's house and found a hermit crab crawling up my leg."

"You know," she told him, "these things must be a lot hardier than I thought." She stifled a giggle at his look of pure bewilderment. "You must not have kids."

"I don't." He sent her a repressive glance. "Could we get back to the subject?"

"Of course. Let's simplify things. Forget it."

He opened his mouth, then shut it with a snap and glared at her. "Are you refusing because I pi—ticked you off? It's childish at the very least to let a personal bias stop you from doing some real good."

Piper shook her head. "You haven't thought this through, and that's because you don't believe my herbs could have cured Randy. Think about it. What if it works? What happens then?"

Publicity happened then, she thought. Lots of publicity. Oh, Lord, if the tabloids got hold of this . . . Determined to convince Chambers to drop the idea, she continued. "Imagine what the tabloids could do with something like this. 'Aphrodisiac Discovered in West Texas.' 'Herbalist Discovers Cure for Impotence.' Never mind that I'm no more an herbalist than Herman is. That's what they'd call me. If they didn't call me something worse. Something like sex herbalist, probably." That kind of innuendo she didn't need. Couldn't deal with. Not with her past.

Piper closed her eyes at the sudden rush of memories. An image filled her mind, as clear as the day she'd first seen the papers. Headlines screaming her name, a picture of herself on the courthouse steps. God, not again, she thought, shaking the image away.

Leaving Herman on the counter, she paced the room. "It would be a zoo. A nightmare. Everybody and their dog would descend on the area and all the peace would be shot straight to hell." Especially her peace. Once the media found out who had invented the remedy, her past would again be fodder for the rumor mills. Lord, she couldn't bear to imagine it. She had her son to think of now.

"Beautiful herbalist," Chambers murmured with a glint in his eyes.

Her attention caught, she stared at him. "Pardon me?"

"I said, beautiful herbalist. 'Beautiful Herbalist Discovers Cure for Impotence.'"

She flushed again and her stomach fluttered. Lord, the man was flirting with her. A tingle of excitement crept up the back of her neck. Ruthlessly, she squashed it.

"Nursery owner," she corrected him severely. "Not an herbalist." She returned to her original point, warming to the theme. "That's only the beginning. The possibilities for abuse are endless. What if the crime lords got hold of it?"

"Why don't you let me worry about that?" he said. "I can absolutely guarantee I won't sell it to any crime lords."

The easy smile he gave her invited her to share the joke. It made him look younger, even better looking. He wasn't drop-dead gorgeous, but that charm was lethal. His light brown hair had fallen forward over his brow. She didn't know why, but it disarmed her, made her want to push his hair back from his forehead, like she did her son's. Piper decided Eric Chambers was about as guileless as a rattler.

"Well, Ms. Stevenson. What's it going to be?"

"The answer is no," she said, and enjoyed his look of disbelief.

"How can you refuse? Surely you can see the importance of researching this remedy."

"Nope." Important or not, she couldn't risk it. "All I see is that you can't guarantee that the remedy won't be misused and you can't promise that my part in finding this supposed aphrodisiac won't get out to the press. No research is important enough for me to risk the negative publicity. I'm thinking about my son, Dr. Chambers, and that's the only decision I can make. You can leave now."

"Wait!"

She slanted him a haughty look. "Wait for what? We have nothing left to discuss."

"The hell we don't. If you think I'm getting into a moving vehicle with Gus the Grim again, you're absolutely nuts."

"Gus the Grim? Gus drove you here?" What was he talking about?

"After my car broke down he picked me up. He must be in cahoots with the grim reaper. Probably brings him sacrificial victims by scaring them to death with his driving."

Laughing in spite of herself, she said, "Your metaphors are a bit mixed. The grim reaper doesn't have sacrificial victims."

"Literature was never my forte. Isn't there another way I can get home? Like call a cab?" he suggested hopefully.

"Sorry. No can do. No cabs."

"Then I'll walk."

"It's twelve or fifteen miles to Capistrano. Unless you're a marathon runner, it will take you forever to get there."

"I run," he said, adding at her skeptical look, "Well, maybe not fifteen miles at a time, but I do run."

"Oh, all right, I'll give you a ride," she said reluctantly. "I have some errands in Capistrano."

"Lifesaver isn't too strong a word. Thank you."

Watch out, Piper, she told herself. This man was no dummy. Now that he'd decided he couldn't get that remedy one way, he'd try to get it another. And she was just dumb enough to let him charm her.

"Let me make a couple of calls and we can go." She dialed, her fingers tapping a staccato rhythm on the counter while she waited for her grandfather to pick up his cellular phone. "Grandpa? You're supposed to have the phone on you, you know. What good will it do you if you can't reach it?"

Piper held the receiver away from her. Though Charlie Stevenson's words weren't discernible, the tenor of the reply boomed across the airwaves. "Yeah?" She brought the receiver back against her ear. "Well you just listen to me, you cantankerous old coot—" She broke off, grinning. "Promise to keep it beside you next time and I'll back off. I wasn't calling to check on you. I've got to go to Capistrano. Cole is at Jason's. See you later."

Another call to Jason's mother and she was ready to go.

Stepping over the slumbering dog at the foot of the steps, Eric followed Piper across the yard. "Look, I'm sorry if I came on a little strong."

"Strong? Try rude, obnoxious, or offensive."

Eric didn't think he'd been that bad, but it would only antagonize her more to say so. Diplomatically he said, "I'm sure you wouldn't intentionally do anything to harm Mr. Johnson, but he is my patient, and I'm responsible for his health. Randy's improvement and Virginia's subsequent pregnancy mean a lot to both of them, and when they told me about you . . ." He shrugged. "I'll admit I was skeptical."

"Think nothing of it," she said with an airy wave of her hand. "I'm used to being insulted by perfect strangers."

Did that smart mouth of hers ever get her into trouble? "Good, then I won't worry."

For a moment she stared at him, then she laughed. "Got me on that one."

Pleased, he started to answer, then choked and cut himself off, staring at the vehicle in front of him.

Another pickup, worse than Gus's. The rear end was a study in dent art. Large, small, some of them old and rusted, others obviously newer, they were a collage of indentations. *Oh, God*, he thought, *I should have taken my chances with Gus.*

He cleared his throat. "Tell me something, Piper. Are the dents in the pickup all yours?"

TWO

Eric didn't miss the amused look Piper sent him, or the laugh she tried to cover with a cough. "No," she answered as she gestured for him to climb in. "I can't take credit for them. This is my grandfather's truck." She cranked the engine, jammed the gearshift into reverse, and backed out of the gravel drive at Mach speed, narrowly avoiding a small bush.

Eric clung to the dashboard. "How old is your grandfather?"

"Oh, it's not age that makes him that way; he's always done that to trucks. He doesn't look behind him when he backs up." She shifted gears and pressed on the accelerator.

"He backs up without looking behind him?" What kind of nut backed up without looking behind him?

"Yep. Just puts his foot to the floor and away he goes."

"That's insane. Why doesn't he look behind him?"

"That's Grandpa," she said, shrugging. "All the old ranchers around here do that." Thoughtfully, she added,

"You know, I think it's more like all the ranchers, period. Other than that little quirk, Grandpa's a good driver."

Eric wasn't sure whether she was serious or not. The dents, however, spoke for themselves.

"So tell me, Doctor, how long have you lived in Capistrano and what in the world brought you there?"

"Eric," he said, tired of her calling him "Doctor." "I've lived there about two months. And why shouldn't I live in Capistrano?"

"Just doesn't seem like your kind of town, stuck way out in the middle of Nowhere, Texas."

"Why do you say that?" He shifted and his knees jammed into the dash.

Piper noticed his discomfort. "One of the prices you pay riding with a short person," she said, looking pleased.

Eric eyed the long expanse of her bare legs. They didn't look short. Even ending in a pair of bright pink socks and beat-up tennis shoes, her legs were something to see. Along with the pink socks, she wore lime-green shorts and a yellow T-shirt with the word "Not!" printed on it. Interesting color scheme, he thought.

In answer to his question, she said, "You seem like the big-city type."

It didn't sound like a compliment. His head banged against the window as she swerved to avoid a pothole. He bit off a curse. "Capistrano suits me fine." Much better than Dallas had. Eric liked Capistrano, both the slower pace and the more personalized practice. "Looks like you've got quite an operation going. I thought you only sold herbs until I saw your greenhouse."

"No, the herbs are a sideline. I grow more African violets and orchids than anything else."

He wondered how she could possibly make a living in the middle of "Nowhere, Texas," as she so aptly put it. He glanced out the window, noticing how barren the area was. Barren of people, at least. Cattle, on the other hand, were plentiful.

Piper could have lived in the big city easily, he'd have thought. Clearly, she was no hick from the sticks. But she didn't live in the city. She lived right here on a ranch in the middle of one of the most sparsely populated areas of the state. With her grandfather and her son—and no husband. Knowing she wasn't married didn't break his heart.

Noticing the route she was taking, he asked, "Are you going to Capistrano?"

"Of course. Where did you think I was taking you?"

"Gus came through the mountains."

She bit her lip. "Gus always comes by the mountain road. He likes it."

Eric stared at her, his eyes widening. "He always comes by . . . You mean I didn't have to suffer through that?" A strangled sound escaped him. "That was the worst excuse for a road I ever saw. With Gus driving, it defies description." He shuddered, remembering.

"Think what an experience, though," she said with only the barest hint of a laugh in her voice.

"Experience? 'Nightmare on Elm Street' is more like it." Eric lapsed into silence. A memory niggled at the corners of his mind, something to do with her name, but he couldn't quite place it. "My mother is into plants," he said after a minute. "In fact, she raises African violets.

She's been bugging my father to build her a greenhouse for them for about a year now. Since she's taken over half the living room with plant stands and grow lights, I suspect he'll do it before too much longer."

"That's how I started. I bullied Grandpa and Sam, our ranch foreman, into building my first greenhouse when I was ten. Are you interested in plants?"

"Don't know too much about them, other than the times I go looking for a present for my—" The elusive memory became clear. "Now I remember. You're 'Pay the Piper,' aren't you? The name should have tipped me off."

She turned a long, slow smile on him. "You've heard of me?"

A woman with a smile like that was dangerous. "Saw some of your plants in a nursery in San Antonio when I was looking for a present for my mother. Why didn't you tell me?"

"You didn't ask about my nursery. You were too busy shouting at me about my herbal remedy, remember? If I *were* an herbalist, I do believe I'd be insulted. Do you have a hang-up about herbalists or something?"

"Not at all." His legs were cramping and he shifted them again. "I merely said I didn't think you should practice medicine without a license."

"Since I wasn't practicing medicine, that's a moot point, isn't it?"

"No." He stretched his legs toward the door and angled his shoulders closer to her.

Piper stared at him. "What do you mean, no?"

"We haven't established that anything is a moot point, and we won't until you tell me what's in that remedy." He smiled when she started to sputter. "Better watch the road," he advised. "I'm not quite as narrow-minded as you seem to think, Piper. And I thought you were going to call me Eric."

"I didn't say you were narrow-minded." She shot him a sidelong glance. "Eric," she added in dulcet tones.

"You didn't need to. Piper."

She laughed, abandoning the subject. "I'm surprised you've heard of me. I ship to several places in Texas, but it's a wholesale operation, and fairly limited."

"Chatty sales clerk," he said. "She said your plants weren't typical of what I'd find in other nurseries."

A delighted smile lit her face. "Oh, that's wonderful! That's exactly what I try for. I can't compete in volume yet, so I try to make up for it with unusual species."

Eric smiled, enjoying her enthusiasm. "Apparently you're succeeding."

"Well, I hope so. We're getting near town. Where do you want me to drop you off?"

"The garage, if you don't mind. Hopefully they've got a tow truck for my car. That's the third time I've broken down since I moved here. The garage can't manage to fix it."

"Oh, some foreign job? What did you expect in a town the size of a peanut? A Mercedes dealership?"

"Every doctor drives a foreign sports car, right?"

"Some of them drive Cadillacs," she returned, impudently.

"Well, it is foreign. It's a seven-year-old Toyota, and believe me, it's not by any stretch a sports car." He paused a moment and added, "My ex-wife has the sports car."

"You're divorced?"

Why did she sound so surprised? He nodded. "For a couple of years now." He started to ask her the same question, but she spoke before he could.

"Granville's Garage," she said, pulling into a tiny service station on the corner of Main and Piccolo. She waved at the old men sitting out in front of the barbershop across the street, who were staring at them with interest.

Eric walked around the truck and rested his forearm on her open window frame. "Thanks for the ride. My nerves thank you for the ride. Do you come into Capistrano often?"

She nodded. "It's the closest town. If I need something besides staples, I go into Alpine or Fort Davis."

A stray breeze ruffled her blond hair, making him wonder if it felt as soft as it looked. Her mouth curved in a warm, kissable smile. It struck him that spending time with Piper might be just what he needed, now that he'd gotten rid of the bad taste his divorce had left. The thought had probably been in the back of his mind since he first set eyes on her, he realized.

Well, why not? Nothing was wrong with asking a pretty woman out, he assured himself. All beautiful women weren't like his ex-wife, Dawn. A date with Piper didn't mean he was considering a serious relationship anytime soon. He merely wanted a little female companionship. Besides, he still needed the remedy. Getting to know her better could only help his cause.

"Eric?"

With a start, he realized he'd been staring at her.

"Are you all right? You looked kind of funny for a minute."

"Sorry. Daydreaming." If he asked her out now, she'd turn him down, suspecting he only wanted the remedy. He'd do better to wait. "Thanks again," he said, and left her.

Eric reached for the phone, hesitating once more before he picked it up. A couple of days had passed since he'd met Piper Stevenson. Long enough, he figured, to make her wonder why he hadn't called—assuming she'd thought about him at all. He suspected she had. Hoped she had, anyway.

It's just a date, he thought, picking up the phone and dialing her number. He'd take her out, get to know her a little better, set her at ease enough to get the dry-skin formula from her. If they hit it off and something more . . . physical happened, then great.

He dropped the phone back into the cradle before the connection went through. Standing, he paced the length of his office, halting at the window to stare out at a small courtyard. What was his problem? It was a date, nothing more. Just because Piper was a beautiful woman didn't mean she was another Dawn. Oh, for Pete's sake, lighten up, he told himself. He wasn't thinking about marrying her. Taking her to bed, however . . . that was a whole different subject. It had been a long time since he'd been intimate with a woman. And Piper was very tempting.

Eric again picked up the phone and dialed her number.

❖————————❖

Piper put the orchid cutting down and glanced out the opened window of the greenhouse, wondering where her son had gone. His bike stood abandoned in the middle of the yard, and Cole was nowhere to be seen. Neither was Jumbo, but then the dog usually went where Cole did. Part of her thoughts were on the trouble her son might be getting into, part on the orchid hybrid she was pruning, but the major portion of them centered on Eric Chambers.

Two days earlier he'd walked into her greenhouse and demanded she tell him about her dry-skin formula. Concerned for his patient, determined to find out about the remedy, he hadn't struck her as a man who would give up easily. So why, when she refused to give him the list of ingredients, had he accepted her decision and forgotten all about it? And all about her? That was the crux of the problem. He was the first man in ages she'd been the tiniest bit interested in, and he hadn't even called her.

Well, why hadn't he? Even if she didn't date often, she knew when a man found her attractive. And Eric had definitely acted interested. In the formula, she reminded herself, not necessarily in her.

Oh, why did she care? Even if he asked her, she wouldn't go out with him. Piper knew better than to let another charming doctor get to her. She had the scars to prove what a disaster that could be.

The phone rang, interrupting her thoughts. "Yuck," she said as she smeared mud down the side of her face when she picked up the receiver.

"Yuck? Is that a west Texas way to answer the phone?"

"Who is this?" Her heart rate speeded up, her stomach tensed with nerves. She'd known who it was the instant she'd heard that smooth, bass voice, but she didn't want him to know that.

"It's Eric Chambers."

"Oh. Hi." As much to distract herself from the annoying rhythm of her heart rate as to check on her son, Piper craned her neck to look out the window again. Still no sign of him.

Eric went on. "I hear there's a steak house in Alpine with the best food around. Would you like to go with me?"

"Go with you?" she repeated blankly.

"Yes, to dinner, Friday night."

She frowned, instantly suspicious. "You're just trying to get the formula from me."

"So untrusting. Do you really think I'd ask you out just to get the formula?"

"Yes."

He laughed. "You underrate yourself. No formula talk, I swear."

"You mean, like a date?" Oh, no. She couldn't do it. Could she?

"Just like a date. Is that a problem?" Though his tone was serious now, she could hear suppressed laughter in his voice.

"Not a problem exactly, but I don't date . . . often." Dammit, what was wrong with her? She'd been doing fine until she added the qualifier.

"I'd really like to take you out." His deep, sincere

voice sent a chill up her spine and prickles of anticipation surging along her skin.

Sincerity. It weakened her resistance, as if she weren't having enough trouble already. "Well . . ." Tempted, but still apprehensive, she hesitated. Her gaze drifted back outside. "Hang on a minute," she told him, and abandoned the phone to rush to the window and yell at Cole.

"Sorry," she said on her return. "They say God made children cute because otherwise we'd kill them. If my son didn't have cute down to a fine art, he'd be dead a hundred times over by now."

"What did he do?"

Piper shifted her weight, shoulder to the wall. "He was about thirty seconds away from setting a bonfire."

"A bonfire? How did he get hold of matches?"

"Half the help on the ranch smoke," she said defensively. "They leave matches everywhere. Have you ever taken care of a six-year-old boy?"

"Can't say that I have. Not alone, anyway."

"Try it sometime. It would be a real education for you." Cole came barreling down the long aisle of the greenhouse, gravel spewing from beneath his tennis shoes. Halting in front of her, he began demanding answers to fifteen different questions.

"I'm sure it would be," Eric said. "What about Friday?"

Attempting to listen to Eric, Piper glared at her son and held her finger to her mouth. Cole ignored her, starting a litanous chant along the lines of "What's for dinner? Can I have ice cream?"

In her other ear, Eric was still talking, though she

missed most of what he was saying. He was the most tenacious man. She wondered what he'd do if she refused again. "Hush," she mouthed at Cole, considering grounding him for life. Or at least the next half hour.

Irritated, frustrated by the stubbornness and pure orneriness of men both young and old, she told Eric, "Oh, all right. Friday is fine."

"Great. I'll pick you up at six."

How had that happened? she asked herself as she hung up the phone. She'd had no intention of dating again. Especially not a slick doctor. It was Cole's fault, she decided. And that smooth talker, Eric Chambers. If her son hadn't been driving her to distraction on one side while Eric persevered on the other, she never would have agreed.

When Friday night arrived, Piper reasoned that she couldn't very well wear shorts and a T-shirt to dinner, so she put on her newest outfit, a soft peach skirt and a blouse of the same color. She still wasn't sure how she'd let Eric talk her into going out with him. She wandered into the kitchen to wait for him and heard the door bang shut a few seconds later.

Charlie Stevenson came in, threw his hat in the general direction of the counter, and collapsed in a chair. "Damn, that new stallion is something else. If his stud fees weren't going to bring us some good money, I'd be tempted to sell him." He looked at Piper hopefully. "Any beer in the fridge?"

Guiltily, she said, "Sorry, Grandpa, I forgot. Look, if he's so bad, let's just get rid of him."

"Santana's the best cutting-horse stud I've seen in years. We can't afford to let him go. You know he's worth a lot more as a stud than he would be if we sold him. And we need the new blood for our line. He's not that bad, just a little ornery. Your grandpa's gettin' old, honey, that's all."

"You're not old." To Piper, Charlie had always seemed ageless. "Let the new hand deal with Santana." Even as she made the suggestion, she knew it was useless.

"Ha! Some help he is. He's about as much good as a milk bucket under a bull." Charlie shook his head in disgust.

"So fire him and hire someone else. Lord knows you and Sam could use some more help. Especially during the summer when you're breeding most of the mares."

"Easier said than done. I still need to hire another man anyway. If we had a hand who knew something, then we could make do with three of us. The longhorns pretty much take care of themselves, but . . ." His voice trailed off and his gaze focused on Piper. "Now I see why you didn't get any beer. Your big date must've pushed it out of your mind. Are you sure you know what you're doing? I thought you didn't even like this fella. He's a doctor, isn't he?"

"Grandpa, I hope I'm not so prejudiced that I dislike all doctors."

"Wouldn't be a wonder if you did. After what that sorry son of a—"

Piper interrupted him before he could get too wound up. "I've been over him for a long time now."

Charlie snorted, looking doubtful. "Well, you always

did have more guts than you could hang on a fence. Remember when you decided you were gonna break Stomper?" He laughed and shook his head. "Every time that horse threw you, you climbed right back on until you finally showed him who was boss."

"Had to. You and Sam would never have let me hear the end of it."

"Stubbornness and courage will take you a long way, girl. Wasn't the first or last time I've been proud of you, either."

Surprised at the sudden sentimentality from the crusty old rancher, she made light of it. "Guess you're getting forgetful in your old age. Last week you said I was the cussedest female you'd ever known."

Charlie bristled, started to argue, but then smiled. "Crafty little thing, leading me off the scent like that. Tell me why you're going out with a fella you said you had no use for."

"I didn't say that. Besides, it's just dinner."

"Just dinner," her grandfather repeated, his eyes twinkling. "Then why are you wearing a skirt? And isn't that a new blouse?"

"I've had it for months," she lied without a blush. "Thanks for staying with Cole."

Charlie grunted. "About time you started going out again. All you ever do is work on those danged plants of yours. Last time you went out was—"

She held up a hand to cut him off. "If this time's as bad as that, I'm swearing off men forever." How could she date when there weren't any single men close to her age around here. And the last time she went out of town and had a date, he competed for the title of "Most Boring." Until he took her back to her hotel. She hoped he was still limping. "Dr. Chambers is just trying to get on my good side so I'll tell him what I put in that herbal recipe."

"You think that's what this is about?" Charlie asked her. "He could've gone about it another way, if that's all he wanted."

"Your imagination is working overtime, Grandpa. Even if he was interested, I'm not. I'm not looking to get involved with another doctor. Or any man, for that matter."

"Then why are you going out with him?"

The doorbell rang and Piper hurried to get it, relieved she wouldn't have to answer Charlie. She had asked herself the same question fifty times, and she still hadn't come up with a satisfactory answer.

The steak house in Alpine combined good food, cold beer, and loud country music, providing better entertainment than almost anywhere else around. Smoky, loud, crowded, it wasn't a scene for seduction, which suited Piper fine.

The hostess slapped two ice-cold mugs of beer on the table with a sloshing, dish-rattling thud and disappeared as quickly as she had come. Enormous heads foamed up, spilling over the sides of the mugs. Piper grabbed the saltshaker and threw a pinch of salt into her brew, killing the head instantly.

Realizing Eric was staring, she said, "Have some salt. Gives it a good flavor too." She took a healthy sip and set the mug down, satisfied.

"A true beer drinker, are you?" he asked, smiling.

It really wasn't fair, she decided, that he had such a great smile. Fortunately, it didn't affect her . . . much. "Just a country girl at heart, Doc," she drawled, crossing one leg over the other and lounging back in her chair.

"Have you always lived around here?"

She nodded. "Except for college."

"Where did you go?" A beeper went off, and Eric's hand dropped to his belt.

Disappointment shot through her, more than she wanted to feel. "Well, it's been fun."

"Habit," he said. "It's not mine, but whenever I hear one, I think it's for me."

"I've read that in the cities drug dealers carry them."

"Thanks a lot."

She laughed. "I just meant it's funny how many different people use them now."

"That's true. I'll try not to take offense at being compared to a drug dealer. Of course, you already suspect me of being in league with crime lords."

She gaped at him. "I never said that."

He cocked an eyebrow. "No?"

"That's not . . . I didn't mean . . . What I meant . . . ," she stammered and suddenly stopped. Her eyes narrowed and she glared at him. "You knew I didn't think that."

"Yeah, but it was impossible to resist." He smiled at her again. "Come on, Piper. A minute ago you compared me to a pusher."

Her voice rose with her frustration. "I did not!"

"Say, Piper, this fella botherin' ya?"

A sunburned older man in a beat-up straw cowboy

hat towered massively over their table. Oh, Lord, it would be, she thought. "Sam. What are you doing here?"

"I'd surely love to help you, darlin', seein's how Charlie ain't around. Do I need to take this fella outside and learn him some manners?" Hitching up his pants, he leaned closer to Eric.

She risked a glance at Eric, who was struggling not to laugh. Her irritation faded as quickly as it had flared. "That's okay, Sam. It's nothing. This is Eric Chambers, the new doctor from Capistrano. Eric, meet Sam Buckner."

Sam snorted. "Charlie know you're out with this"—he looked Eric up and down—"this doctor fella?"

Piper choked down her exasperation. It never did any good with Sam, who was even more protective of her than Charlie was. "Sam's the foreman on the ranch," she explained to Eric. "He seems to have forgotten I'm a grown woman."

"Ain't forgot it. Grown women need pertectin' more'n young 'uns, *if* you catch my drift. I'm settin' right over there." Motioning at a table with a sweep of his brawny arm, he pinned Eric with a warning glare and stalked off.

Eric watched him go, a smile tugging at his mouth, then turned to Piper. "Now I've been put properly in my place. Something tells me I wouldn't want to tangle with Sam."

"Well . . ." Her cheeks dimpled in a smile. "Sam might be old, but he's tough as boot leather."

"I don't doubt it." He reached out and covered one of her hands with his. "Truce?"

His light touch sent a sparkle of excitement flowing through her bloodstream. Bewildered by the unexpected strength of the sensation, she raised her eyes to find him smiling at her. His eyes, she realized, changed color with his feelings. Although gray at times, right now they glowed a deep ivy-green, with no gray in them at all. Her heart thumped in a staccato rhythm and she felt breathless, like she did when one of her hybrid experiments turned out successfully. "Truce," she agreed.

He released her hand. "So, where did you go to school?"

Thankfully, her breathing evened out. "Texas Tech."

"Lubbock's a nice town. I've got some friends who live there. What's your degree in?"

Friends in Lubbock? Oh, God, she couldn't possibly be that unlucky, could she? Piper felt her color rising and cursed silently. "I majored in horticulture, but I didn't finish my degree." She took a sip of beer, her fingers tightening on the mug. "My life took an . . . unexpected turn my junior year."

"Sorry, I didn't mean to bring up painful subjects."

"It's not anymore," she said, shrugging. *Liar*, she thought. It still hurt every bit as much today as it did then.

Eric studied her for a minute. "You knew from the first that you wanted a career with plants? A lot of people don't have a clue about what they want when they hit college."

"I've had a thing about plants all my life. Grandpa still has a hard time believing you can make any money from it, but he's always been supportive."

"Can you?" Eric asked. "Make money?"

"Well . . ." She grimaced. "Not much. So far, any-way. I'm trying to expand, so I've been hitting the shows in the larger cities. If I can make contacts there, I can ship to them. Unfortunately, though, my expansion is limited by my lack of capital." How did he do it? she wondered. Was he really that interested in what she said, or was it a talent of his to make a woman feel that she fascinated him?

"Have you thought about getting a loan?"

His smile said "trust me." She didn't, not for a min-ute. But it was fun talking to a man whose eyes didn't glaze over at the mention of her business. Answering his question, she nodded ruefully. "Sure. The local bank wouldn't go for it unless my grandfather cosigned. Not that he wouldn't have done it," she hastened to assure him, "but it's hard enough making a go of breeding cut-ting horses. I couldn't let Grandpa take that risk."

"I had the impression your grandfather's operation is fairly large."

"Medium-sized. He's down to about two hundred acres now that he runs longhorns on. The cutting-horse operation is his main source of income. He's just gotten a new stud that we're excited about."

"You could try another bank," Eric suggested. "One that would give you the loan on the merit of your busi-ness alone."

"I could, but I decided against it rather than risk overextending myself. I'll just have to take it slow, which probably isn't a bad idea given the present economic climate in Texas."

"You've got a point there." He stroked his finger down the side of his beer mug, and Piper found herself watching that strong, competent hand, wondering what it would feel like if he were to—

"Why African violets and orchids?" he asked, interrupting her wayward thoughts.

She forced herself to concentrate on the subject. What was the matter with her? She hardly knew him. Think plants, not sex, she ordered herself. "I got into them by chance. When I was a child I visited an African violet nursery in Dallas. It was love at first sight."

"What about the herbs?"

She frowned. "I thought you said tonight wasn't about the formula?" She should have known he had an ulterior motive when he asked her out. So much for her idea that he might be interested in *her*.

"It's not," he said, smiling at her. "But that doesn't mean I'll drop the subject forever, Piper, even if we don't talk about it tonight."

"It won't do any good to badger me."

"Don't you think we could have a civil discussion about the formula without my badgering you?"

"I don't know." No, he wouldn't badger. More likely he'd try to charm it out of her. The knowledge that he might be successful irritated her.

"No badgering and no more formula talk," he said. "All right?"

She agreed and let the subject drop. As they sat in silence for the next few minutes, studying their menus, Piper noticed that Eric kept glancing over her shoulder. "What are you looking at?" she finally asked.

"An older woman sitting behind you. She keeps staring at us."

Turning, Piper encountered a malevolent glare. Oh,

great, she thought, facing Eric again. Just what she needed. "That's Mrs. Croaker. Ignore her. She always does that."

"Piper! Long time no see," their waitress said as she reached the table. She cracked her gum and winked. "What've you been up to?"

"Hi, Marge." Silently, she blessed Marge's timing. "Work."

Marge took their order, popping her gum while she wrote. "Got it. Back in a jiff," she said, winking again as she left.

Eric's gaze strayed once more to Mrs. Croaker. He seemed about to say something, but Piper spoke hastily. "Did you always know you wanted to be a doctor?"

He glanced at her. "Pretty much. My uncle was a doctor. We were close, so I grew up around medicine."

"Were you one of those intense premed students in college?"

"You have to be kind of intense to get into med school."

"Where did you do your training?" She wasn't just asking to distract him. She wanted to know more about him.

"Galveston for medical school, San Antonio for residency. Then I practiced in Dallas for several years."

"Why did you move from Dallas?"

He didn't look entirely happy when he answered. "I wanted a change from the university system. I'd been in it since I started in medicine and I wanted more patient contact. When the opportunity in Capistrano came up, I took it."

They talked for a while longer and then Marge returned, tilting Eric's plate back just before the contents landed in his lap. She slammed it on the table with an "Oops, sorry," and slapped Piper's dish down in front of her.

"That was close." Eric viewed his lap with relief before glancing up. "Looks like your friend is coming over."

"Hello, Piper," Mrs. Croaker said in a voice that matched her name. Piper stared at her in silence. "Same poor manners, I see. Aren't you going to introduce me?"

"No," Piper said. She wouldn't pretend to be friendly. Eric gave her a curious look.

Mrs. Croaker sniffed and said to Eric, "I'm Mrs. Blair Croaker." Her rather protuberant eyes bulged.

"Eric Chambers." He shook the hand she thrust forward.

"Chambers? The new doctor in Capistrano?" Her mouth formed a smirking smile that Piper imagined she thought was pleasant.

"That's right."

"We've heard so much about you. My daughter-in-law is having a baby and wants you to be her doctor. Their second child," she said, with a pointed look at Piper. "And you so new to town and you've already met Piper. What a *coincidence*." Her tone was one of honeyed venom. "Did you know each other before you came here, Doctor? Perhaps in Lubbock?"

"Excuse us," Piper interrupted, "our dinner's getting cold."

For a moment Mrs. Croaker looked like she wasn't

going to leave, but then she sniffed again and said, "Nice to meet you, Doctor."

"What was that about?" Eric asked after she left. "She seemed a little strange."

"Not strange, just plain mean." Piper stared after the older woman. "I used to be engaged to her son and it didn't work out. Ever since then she's hated me." Hate was a mild description of how Neil Croaker's mother felt about her.

"In that case, we'll just forget her," he said.

Piper wished it were that simple. Don't be stupid, just tell him, she tried to convince herself. You know he'll find out eventually. Better if he hears it from you than from her.

Oh, what difference did it make what Mrs. Croaker or anyone else told him? She wasn't going to get involved with him, so what he heard or didn't hear shouldn't matter a bit.

"Don't you ever miss the city?" she asked, determined to avoid thinking about Mrs. Croaker. Why should she let that old biddy ruin the first date she'd had in months?

"Not much. All I have to do is remind myself of the traffic, the smog, the crime—"

"Stop," she said, laughing. "Okay, I'll admit Capistrano does have some advantages."

"And some I hadn't even realized," he added, taking her hand in his again.

She'd walked right into that one. Her heart gave a skip and her stomach fluttered at the contact. She was being foolish, letting herself be affected by him. A man who could make a place like the steak house seem romantic was definitely trouble. But why couldn't she pretend, just for tonight? It was a refreshing change, being with a charming man who knew nothing of her past.

He squeezed her hand lightly before releasing it. If she hadn't been a practical woman, she'd have sworn her hand tingled.

They finished eating and Eric waved at Marge. "Early day tomorrow," he said to Piper. "Do you mind?"

"That's all right. On a ranch all the days start early." As they left, Piper noticed he gave Marge a good tip, even after she'd nearly dumped his dinner in his lap.

They didn't talk on the way home until Eric broke the silence to ask her a question. "Is something wrong?"

Surprised, she looked at him. "No. Why do you ask?"

"You're quiet." He patted her hand that rested on her knee. A comforting gesture, but there was nothing comfortable in the bone-melting jolt she felt at his touch. "It was that woman, wasn't it? Anything you want to talk about?"

Oh, Lord, he sounded so sympathetic. "No, it's nothing." She hadn't been thinking of Mrs. Croaker, she'd been thinking about Eric. About kissing him good night. Even before they turned into the driveway, anticipation made her stomach churn. Why in the world was she making a big deal out of a simple good-night kiss?

He walked her to the door, but instead of leaving, he simply stood there staring at her. At her mouth. He was going to kiss her. She wanted him to. And she was scared witless of what would happen when he did.

"Good night, Piper. I'll call you."

She watched him leave, deflating like a popped balloon. All that buildup for nothing. Her hand balled into a fist. She'd bet dollars to donuts Eric had planned it that way.

THREE

Eric's receptionist was out with a virus, her replacement couldn't spell hello and couldn't count past ten, and Mrs. Croaker waited in the exam room. A perfect Monday morning.

"What seems to be the problem today?" Eric asked Mrs. Croaker, hoping she wouldn't be as unpleasant as he remembered from the other night.

"Oh, Dr. Chambers, my allergies have been just terrible lately," she complained, putting a hand to her sizable nose.

His attempts at taking a history were hindered by her comments about the citizens of Capistrano. She knew everyone and she wanted to talk about everyone. Time and again he brought the subject back to her health. Time and again, she launched into yet another story, most of them vituperative. Halting Mrs. Croaker in full swing was as futile as trying to stop a tidal wave.

Finally, she worked around to Piper, whom he suspected she'd come to tell him about in the first place. Once more, he tried to head her off. "It's quite inappropriate for you to be telling me all this," he said. "Many of these people are my patients. When they want me to know something, they'll tell me."

"Poor Charlie," she continued, undaunted. "When Piper turned up pregnant and not a husband in sight—bold as you please for all the world to see—it like to have killed him. She's all he's got left." Her eyes gleamed with malice, sparkled with pleasure at spreading the gossip. "Shameless, that's what she is. Thank the Lord my Neil found out before she trapped—"

Eric had had enough. "You should see a specialist in Fort Stockton, Mrs. Croaker. I'm afraid I can't help you." He opened the door and stared at her, waiting for her to leave.

She didn't move. "Blood will tell, I always say. When Tanner Stevenson—he was Charlie's only child—married that woman, I knew there'd be hell to pay. With an immoral mother like hers, is it any wonder Piper took up with—"

Eric closed her file with a snap and walked out, leaving her with her fishlike mouth hanging open. People like her made him sick. Though she'd had no compunction about maligning everyone, smearing Piper had given her special pleasure.

Piper hadn't said, but Eric had assumed she'd married young and then divorced. To find out she'd never been married was a surprise, but he'd be the last person to judge her, especially when he didn't know the true story. After all, he'd made some mistakes himself—marrying Dawn had been a doozy. No, he admired Piper for having the guts to raise her son where she wanted to, regardless of malicious small-town tongues. It couldn't have been easy for her to begin with. Add to that people of Mrs. Croaker's ilk and it must be downright miserable at times.

"I told you you didn't have to come out here," Eric said to Dave Burson when he picked him up that afternoon at the Alpine airport.

"The hell I didn't," Dave said. "You're not getting anywhere, so obviously I'll have to attend to it myself. What's the problem? Why won't she give you the formula for the remedy?"

"Piper doesn't want the publicity. And she thinks it could cause problems in the wrong hands." Crime lords, he thought, smiling at their private joke.

"Did you tell her about my clinic?" Dave asked.

"She didn't give me a chance to. She won't give that formula to anyone."

"If you wanted to, you could charm her out of it."

Eric grinned. The formula wasn't what he wanted to charm Piper out of. "Afraid not, Dave. But you're welcome to try."

"What's she like? I'm good with little old ladies."

"Too bad, buddy. She's young."

"I'm even better with them. Is she married?"

"What does that have to do with anything?" Eric asked. Come to think of it, Dave was damn good with young, unattached women.

"So she's not. Do I detect a little interest, Dr. Chambers? I thought you'd sworn off women lately."

"Hardly." Eric flicked him a sardonic glance. "Just because I wouldn't go out on a second date with that vampire you set me up with doesn't mean I have no interest in women."

"Chicken. You have to admit Lila's a knockout."

"You go out with her, then. I've still got teeth marks."

Dave laughed. "I did. That's why I set her up with you."

"With friends like you," Eric said.

Half an hour later, they arrived at the Stevenson ranch. The sleepy dog was nowhere to be seen, and neither was anyone else. Assuming Piper would be in the greenhouse, Eric crossed the yard and pulled open the door. A blast of water hit him full in the face. "What the—" Sputtering, he backed into Dave.

Holding a sprayer, Piper stared at them both with round-eyed dismay. A few feet away, also holding a hose, stood Cole. Both of them were soaking wet.

"Have we come at a bad time?" Eric asked.

She laughed. "Cole was just helping me water. I'm sorry, Eric. Your friend must think I'm a lunatic."

"Well, Dave?" Eric grinned and cocked an eyebrow at his companion.

"Uh, I, uh—" Dave stuttered for several seconds. "Am I to take this as a definite 'no' about sharing your remedy?"

A corner of her mouth lifted in a smile. "Ah, you must be the illustrious Dr. Burson." At Eric's confirmation, she continued. "Eric warned me about you. Give me a minute to change and we'll talk about it. Cole, find some towels for Dr. Chambers and Dr. Burson."

Cole grabbed a couple of towels from the rack of metal shelves standing against one wall and handed them to Dave and Eric. Judging by the number, Eric figured water fights were the norm. After leading them outside to the stone fence, Cole disappeared in the direction of the barn.

Shortly, Piper returned, wearing a dry T-shirt and shorts. Her damp hair curled about her face like a blond halo and she wore no makeup. He wondered how a knockout like Piper apparently had no artifices. Every beautiful woman he'd ever known had worked at it. Dawn, Eric remembered, wouldn't have been caught dead without makeup on. But then, Piper didn't need it.

"No formula," she said immediately to Dave. "I told Eric I wouldn't give it out and I haven't changed my mind."

"Then why did you agree to see me?" Dave asked.

"Because he hangs in there like hair in a biscuit," she said, with a jerk of her thumb at Eric. "He thinks you can convince me to change my mind. So go ahead." She folded her arms across her chest. "Convince me."

Dave tried his best, but she still wouldn't buy it. Her expression did soften when Dave described his urology clinic, which took a special interest in male infertility. Piper was a much softer touch than she liked to let on, Eric thought.

"Look, Dr. Burson," she finally said, "until you can assure me that the remedy won't be abused, then I have to say no. And aside from that, I have no intention of exposing my family to the possible publicity a discovery like this could bring."

"It's Dave, please. The chances of the remedy being

abused are extremely remote. And naturally, your part in its development will be kept confidential. Consider all the people your formula might help."

"Do you honestly think it might work as a remedy for impotence?" She shot Eric a skeptical glance. "Eric doesn't believe it. Why do you?"

"In my opinion, there's a good chance it will work. If not as a cure for impotence, possibly as an aid in another problem. Let me take you to dinner tonight and we'll discuss it further."

"She can't," Eric said. "She's already got a date." Both of them turned to stare at him. Piper looked at him like he was a raving madman. "With me," he added.

Dave frowned. "I have to go back tomorrow. I'd hoped we could resolve this before I left."

"It wouldn't make any difference, Dave," Piper said.

"Will you at least consider it?"

"Look, no matter how much you harangue me, the answer is still no." The look she shot Eric told him not to get his hopes up, either. Before she could speak again, the phone in the greenhouse rang and she ran to answer it.

Eric watched her leave. "I need to talk to Piper for a minute and then we can go," he told his friend.

"You're an unscrupulous dog, Chambers," Dave said. "You didn't have a date with her."

Unabashed, Eric grinned at him. "You notice she didn't contradict me. I'll be back."

Piper hung up the phone and turned to Eric, who was leaning against one of the wooden plant benches with his arms crossed over his chest. Rather than apologetic, he looked amused. "Why the devil did you say we had a date?" she asked.

"Simple," he said, lifting his shoulder. "I didn't want you to go out with Dave."

"Don't you want me to give him the formula?"

"Sure." He walked over and stood in front of her, smiling slightly.

"Then why don't you want me to have dinner with him?" She caught a glimpse of devilishly smiling eyes before he put his hands on her shoulders and kissed her. It didn't last long, but even so, fire shot through her veins as his mouth settled firmly and skillfully over hers.

He lifted his head. "Does that answer your question?"

No, actually it raised a heck of a lot more questions than it answered. "Why did you do that?"

"Impulse?"

"Fat chance. You wouldn't know impulse if it jumped up and bit you in the face."

Eric's eyes flashed. His fingers tightened on her shoulders, then he dragged her against him and his mouth came down on hers again. She knew she should shove him away, but she hesitated and in doing so, lost the will. This time he lingered, his tongue slipping lightly into her mouth, enticing, intriguing, making her wonder why she'd ever imagined he was stuffy. One hand slid from her shoulder to the small of her back, bringing her closer to him. After an endless moment he released her.

They stared at each other. Breathlessly, Piper said, "Okay, so maybe I was wrong."

"Are you going to go out with me tonight?"

Oh, she was tempted. "No," she forced herself to say.

"So you're going with Dave?"

He looked amazingly disappointed. She steeled herself against him. Slick, she thought. Just like . . . "No, I'm not going with either of you."

"Can I do anything to change your mind?" His gaze held hers for a long moment, then dropped to her mouth, lingering, intent.

"No," she said hastily, before she weakened. Her knees wanted to buckle, just from a look, but she wasn't going to give in. She had more sense than that. Eric only wanted the formula, and if he didn't . . . If he wanted something else, then she could really be in trouble.

Piper couldn't concentrate on her work the next couple of days. At the potting bench as usual, she wondered wistfully what would have happened if she'd gone out with Eric. Better not to think about it, she told herself. Better not to remember what kissing him—

"Hello, Piper."

Not the voice of her daydreams, but Neil Croaker, her ex-fiancé. Great, just what she needed. "What do you want?"

"Stopped by to talk to Charlie about that new stud. How Charlie got hold of him I can't figure out. Thought we might make a deal for the stud fee." Neil's gaze took in every detail of her appearance in a long, lecherous appraisal. She wondered what had happened to the sweet boy she'd been engaged to so long ago. Too much of his mother's influence, she decided.

"He's probably in the barn," she said brusquely. "Go on down." Ignoring him, she turned back to her work.

"You're looking good, Piper."

Having learned from experience where the conversation was heading, she didn't reply. Neil strolled over to stand next to her, watching her pot her newest orchid. Dark hair, blue eyes—he was a good-looking man still, and he knew it. As owner of one of the largest ranches in the area, he was a big fish in a little pond. He liked that too.

"Real good," he murmured, running his index finger down her cheek.

Piper jerked away. "Grandpa's in the barn."

"What's wrong, baby? Afraid that old feeling will come back?"

"Not a chance. Forget it, Neil. Go home to your wife. I'm not interested." She forced herself not to jam the orchid into its new home.

"Are you afraid Nadine will find out?" He reached out and put his hand on her neck, leaning down to whisper in her ear. "Shoot, honey, there's ways around that. I have a place nobody knows about."

That she didn't doubt. Neil was notorious for his roving eye. "Stop it," she said, batting his hand away. "What part of 'no' don't you understand?"

He took hold of her arms and jerked her up against him. "Hey, baby, when are you gonna forgive me for marrying Nadine?"

Struggling, she shoved him away from her. "If I had

a brick, I swear I'd hit you with it. Only that wouldn't get through to you either."

"Drop the virtuous act," he said, sidling up next to her again. "Don't forget I know the whole story. You didn't have anything against married men a few years ago, now did you?"

Piper paled, then flushed with anger. "If you think that's smooth, you need to work on your lines. Get out."

"Heard about your new beau. Guess I should'a been a doctor, huh? Then you wouldn't be worried if I was married or not. Maybe you can get yourself pregnant again," he jeered.

Her palm cracked against his cheek with a satisfyingly loud noise, snapping his head back. Eyes narrowed, he rubbed the side of his face and gave her a nasty smile. "Think you'll snare this one? At least he's divorced."

Chest heaving, she started to let fly with her opinion of him, when she heard a voice call out her name.

"Piper?" Walking through the doorway that adjoined the two greenhouse sections, Eric glanced at Neil, then her. "I didn't realize you had a customer. Cole said you were out here."

Wonderful, she thought. It had to be Eric. She knew her face was flaming and could just imagine the conclusion he'd reached.

After another lewd smile at her, Neil turned to Eric. "I'm not a customer. I'm an old friend of Piper's. Neil Croaker. You must be . . ."

"Eric Chambers," he said, but Piper noticed he didn't offer his hand.

"Good-bye, Neil," she said.

He put his finger under her chin and tilted it up. She

knocked his hand away and Neil grinned again. "See you later, Piper." With a nod at Eric, he left.

Neil Croaker, Piper's ex-fiancé, Eric thought. If he could believe Mrs. Croaker, though, not the father of her son. Eric hoped that was true. He hated to think of a cute kid like Cole being related to the piece of scum he'd just met.

Piper lifted her chin and said pugnaciously, "What? Don't stand there and stare at me like I'm an interesting new disease."

He grinned. "Believe me, that's the last thing on my mind when I look at you."

Hands on her hips, she faced him. "Go on, ask me. Aren't you wondering what that was about?"

"No." He shrugged. "The handprint on his cheek pretty much told the story."

Her eyes widened and most of her defiance left. "It's not what you think."

"Piper, it doesn't take an Einstein to figure out that he got fresh and you popped him one." And that Croaker had undoubtedly deserved it.

"Was it so obvious?" She started to turn away.

Laughing, he took her hand and lifted it. "Who'd have thought such a delicate hand hid such strength? You looked like you were about to level him when I walked in."

"If only I had," she muttered, pulling her hand away. "Why are you here?"

"To see if you'd change your mind." Eric had given her a few days to cool off, but he hadn't been able to make himself stay away any longer. She'd begun to haunt his dreams—and not solely in a sexual way. He felt a prickle of uneasiness at the thought, but ignored it.

"I told Dave—"

"About going to dinner with me," he interrupted.

She stared at him as if he were speaking a foreign language. "It's only dinner, Piper. What's the harm?"

"I'm—I'm not dressed."

He smiled, the one designed to set nervous patients at ease. "You look fine to me." Fine wasn't exactly the word. Luscious better described her. Funny thing was, she didn't even work at it. Even in a muddy T-shirt with the hem ripped out, she looked great.

"Then you must need glasses," she said tartly. "I'm covered in mud."

He rubbed her cheek lightly with his thumb. "One small smudge isn't covered in mud." He heard her breath draw in at the contact. Wide, vulnerable eyes gazed up into his. Vulnerable. Damn. He dropped his hand. "But I can find something to do while you change."

"Well . . ." She hesitated, then said, "Cole is going over to Jason's to spend the night, so I guess there's no reason I couldn't."

"Great." He could tell she was still reluctant, but he'd managed to catch her off guard. Which was exactly why he'd stopped by as he had.

"The boys are playing video games, so you can't watch TV," Piper said as they walked to the house. "Grab a beer if you want. I won't be long."

As he rummaged in her refrigerator, Eric wondered if that was true. In his experience, women took forever to get ready. Sipping his beer, he wandered into the living room and watched Cole and his friend Jason play a video game.

Video games, apparently, were not a passive business to these kids. They grunted, they groaned, they screamed and shouted. Their faces contorted in an agony of concentration as they jumped dragons, fired on aliens, and eventually rescued princesses from dark dungeons.

During a lull Jason whispered to Cole, "Who's the dude?"

Cole shrugged. "Some guy my mom knows. He's a doctor, but he didn't even know how to help Herman." He shot Eric a wary look and turned back to the game.

"What level are you on?" Eric asked.

"You know how to play?" Cole asked suspiciously.

Eric set the beer can on the coffee table and said, "Some. My niece and nephew taught me."

Thirty seconds later he was on the floor between the boys with the controls in his hands.

Piper peeked into the living room. All she could see over the back of the sofa was the TV, but she heard the usual sounds that meant the boys were involved with their latest game. Only this time she could swear she heard another voice. A deep male voice that could only be . . . "Eric? What are you doing?"

"Aw, Mom," Cole said, tearing his eyes away from the screen, "don't make him leave yet. He was just showin' us how to—"

"You're playing Nintendo?" she asked him, noticing his sheepish grin.

"Sega, actually," he said, handing the control to Cole and unfolding himself from his position on the floor. "Thanks, guys."

"Man, that was awesome," Jason said.

"Radical," Cole said. "Bet I can beat it too. Me first."

"But I'm company. It's my turn," Jason said, reaching for the controller. They settled the dispute without bloodshed and went back to the game.

"You play video games?" Piper repeated.

"Sure. Why not?"

"Well, I mean . . . You're a doctor."

"Do you think I sit around and read medical journals for fun?" His lips curved upward.

"Don't be ridiculous." Her cheeks dimpled. "I thought you'd play golf."

He leaned his head back and laughed. "I play golf too. But I have a niece and nephew who are on the cutting edge of video technology. They've given me some pointers. And," he said with a modest air, "I happen to be good with my hands."

"I'll bet." Out of nowhere the image hit her of his hands molding a path along her arm, her waist, sliding up to her . . . Hold on, she thought, ruthlessly clamping down on the vision.

"Are we dropping the boys off?" he asked.

Thankful he couldn't read her thoughts, she dragged her gaze from his hands to his face. "Yes, thanks. Lynn's expecting them." She turned to the boys. "If you leave now, you can have brownies after dinner."

The boys were out the door before she could blink.

FOUR

Piper looked across the table at Eric and stifled a sigh. Somehow he'd ferreted out the information that Fort Davis possessed a charming hotel with an enchantingly intimate dining room. She must have been crazy to go out with him again. He'd caught her at a weak moment, she consoled herself.

"Why didn't you tell me about this place?" Eric asked her as they sat down. "Don't you like it?"

"Shhh." She looked around and said, "Of course I like it. Don't let the owner hear you say that, he's a friend of Grandpa's."

"Everyone who lives within a hundred and fifty miles of you is a friend of your grandfather's. It amazes me how many people he knows."

"We've lived here all our lives. What do you expect?"

"Good point. That doesn't mean much in a city. I lived in the same neighborhood for five years and still didn't know all my neighbors."

He looked at his menu then, and Piper did the same,

even though she'd seen it a hundred times. After a few minutes of silence, Eric spoke.

"Not to bring up sore subjects, but have you had a chance to think about what Dave said? His request for your formula?"

She glanced up, surprised that he was pursuing the topic. "The answer's the same. Why are you pleading his cause?"

He reached out and took her hand, toying with her fingers. "Let's say I feel a little obligated."

"Since you lied so that I wouldn't go out with him, you mean?"

Eric winced. "You don't pull any punches, do you?"

She smiled sweetly, slipping her hand from his. Better not to touch him, she thought. Her brain seemed to turn off when she did. "No. I grew up with Grandpa and Sam."

The waiter, whom she'd known all her life, appeared to take their order. "How's your grandaddy, Piper?" he asked, shooting a suspicious glance at Eric.

"Fine, Clint. And how are your grandkids?"

"Growin' fast." He took their order and left, not as talkative as usual since the dining room was busy.

"Dave's doing good things with his clinic," Eric said, returning to the argument. "You could be a part of something that could help thousands of people."

"Or hurt them," she shot back. "My original point is still valid. You and Dave can't guarantee it won't be misused in some way. Besides, I couldn't take the publicity if it turned out to be a cure."

He looked at her curiously. "What's wrong with a

little publicity? It wouldn't hurt your business. In fact, it would help it a lot."

"Not worth it," she said, shaking her head. Would he never give up? "You've done your duty, Eric. Let's drop it, okay?"

He sighed and seemed about to say something more, but was forestalled by a woman's voice.

"Dr. Chambers, Piper. How nice to see you."

Piper glanced up to see Virginia and Randy Johnson standing beside their table. Eric rose and shook hands with Randy. Virginia leaned lightly against her husband, resting her hand on her stomach in the classic mother-to-be pose, although she wasn't showing yet. "Our two favorite people," she said with a warm smile.

Piper almost groaned. She shot Eric a glance and had to bite her tongue at the "I told you so" look he gave her. "You look good, Virginia," she said. "Randy must be treating you right."

"Oh, he is." She glanced lovingly at her husband before she turned to Piper. "You'll never know what this has meant to us, Piper. Isn't that right, honey?"

Randy shuffled his feet and looked down at them. "We're purely grateful to you, Piper, and that's a fact," he mumbled. For Randy, that was a speech. Usually he spoke in sentences of five words or less.

The Johnsons stayed and chatted for a few more minutes, then left to get on with their evening. Piper pinned Eric with a glare. "Did you set that up?"

"No, but I have to admit it's the best argument I can think of. They've had a hard time of it."

"You still don't believe my remedy helped them, though, do you?"

He hesitated. "I'm willing to admit that it's a possibility. Dave wants to make sure. Just think about it," he said when she started to speak.

She wished it was possible to give Dave the formula, but she couldn't afford to draw the media's attention again. Not after the last time. If it had only been herself, she might have risked it, but she had Cole to consider now. Shaking her head she said, "I'm not going to change my mind."

She didn't look happy about it, Eric noticed. Almost as if she wanted to, but couldn't. Again, he wondered just what was so terrible about publicity. Her reaction seemed excessive to him, but he knew when to retreat. And obtaining the formula had taken second place to his other motive in getting to know Piper.

How had a beautiful woman like her stayed hidden away on a ranch in west Texas for most of her life? Piper Stevenson didn't seem like a down-home country girl. On the other hand, though she was self-assured, at least about her business, he sensed a curious naïveté about her. An untouched quality, but with a passion that smoldered underneath.

What would it be like to unlock that passion and watch it explode? Damned good, he suspected.

"What?" she asked. "You're staring at me like I've got two heads."

A good thing she didn't know what he'd really been thinking. "I was wondering about your mysterious past."

She froze. "Mysterious? Why do you say that?"

He wanted to take her hand again, but she'd put it in her lap and was sitting straight up in her chair, looking like she was facing an executioner. "You said your grandfather and Sam raised you and that you lived most of your life around here, but you're not a typical country girl."

The tension drained out of her, and he wondered what she'd thought he was talking about. Cole probably, although he couldn't imagine why she'd think he'd be insensitive enough to press her on that subject.

She smiled wryly. "My mother would be glad to hear you say that. She's worked hard at giving me a more"—she considered a moment—"cosmopolitan view of life."

"Your mother's alive?" he asked, surprised.

"Very much so. My father died when I was two, but Mother—" She stopped and smiled again. "Ever hear of Kimberly Loveland?"

"Loveland Models?" Kimberly Loveland owned and ran the biggest modeling agency in the state. While not as influential as Ford or Wilhelmina, Loveland was big business, headquartering in Dallas. "Kimberly Loveland is your mother?"

Piper inclined her head. "The one and only."

That explained Piper's looks. Her mother was still widely held to be one of the most beautiful women in the world. "Didn't you tell me that you'd always lived around here?"

"And I have. Living with my mother would have been a disaster." She laughed. "No, Mother would have murdered me at a young age if she'd had to deal with me all the time. I was much better off living with Grandpa and visiting my mother."

Kimberly Loveland. Eric remembered the last pic-ture he'd seen of her, on the arm of a man who had to be twenty years her junior. Rumor held that if one laid all of Kimberly's lovers end to end, they'd stretch from New York to California. No mystery about that. Wealth and beauty were powerful magnets.

Piper sighed and settled back into her chair. "Are you up for the whole story?"

"Sure, if you are."

She took a sip of wine and folded her hands on the table in front of her. "My father didn't want to be a rancher. At eighteen he took off for the bright lights. For a while he rode the circuit, but his heart wasn't in it."

"The rodeo circuit? Your mother rode the circuit?"

She rolled her eyes. "Of course not. Good-looking men did. My mother likes good-looking men. She and my father met and they fell madly in love. When my father found out he could make infinitely more money as a male model than as a bronc rider, he squelched his macho upbringing and went for the bucks." Her cheeks dimpled as she smiled. "I wish I could have seen Grandpa's face when he heard that for the first time."

Eric laughed. "I don't imagine that was something your grandfather could understand very easily."

"You ain't just whistlin' Dixie. 'Sissy work' is about the least objectionable term he uses to describe it. Anyway, Grandpa didn't hear from him for about six months and then suddenly he showed up at the ranch with my pregnant mother. They got married and tried to make a go of it here. They were both miserable. When I was about a year old, my mother left. My father lasted a week, then he followed her. They both modeled again, but I don't think their marriage was a very happy one. About a year later, my father was killed in a car wreck."

"They just left you with your grandfather?" He tried to imagine either of his parents doing that, but he couldn't.

"I was happy here, and I saw them occasionally. Grandpa's a better parent than either of them could ever have been."

She said the last fiercely. Eric reached out and covered her hands. "Do you ever see your mother now?"

"Since I've grown up, I see her quite a bit." She smiled again, relaxing. "Mother doesn't understand how I can live here. She keeps trying to get me interested in the modeling industry."

"It does seem like you would have experimented with it. You never wanted to be a model?"

"For about thirty seconds. I'm too tall to model petites and too short to be a regular model. And I'd never be thin enough. I'm built on sturdier lines."

"Sturdy isn't the word I'd use," Eric said, looking at her. Voluptuous maybe. Sinful. She made him think of satin sheets and sin. He brought one of her hands to his lips and gently kissed the knuckles. Her scent, as rare and delicate as one of her orchids, assaulted his senses.

"What—what are you doing?" She sounded breathless, he noticed, pleased.

Her pulse beat a wild flutter when he turned her hand over and grazed his lips across her wrist. Hiding a smile, he answered her. "Changing the subject."

"Well—well, don't." She tried to pull her hand loose, but he kissed her wrist again. He heard her moan, a tiny, soft sound he nearly missed.

His lips traveled to her open palm. "Don't what?"

"For heaven's sake, we're in a restaurant," she hissed.

"I know. If we weren't, I wouldn't be kissing just your hand." Dropping a last kiss on her hand, he regretfully let go, gazing at her mouth and schooling his features into an innocent expression.

"Stop trying to—to seduce me," she whispered loudly.

A slow smile spread over his face. "Now that's an intriguing thought. We're in a restaurant, Piper. Even though it's a lot more"—he paused, looked around—"intimate than the steak house, it's still a little too public for my tastes. Assuming I was attempting to seduce you, of course."

The waiter chose that moment to reappear at their table to see if they needed anything. He seemed inclined to linger and chat with Piper, but Eric finally got rid of him by asking for the check.

"Now where were we, Angel?"

"Leaving. You asked for the check, remember?"

He grinned and after paying, led her out. On the way home he kept the conversation light and general. His thoughts were anything but, and he suspected hers weren't either.

"Grandpa forgot to leave the porch light on," she said as they pulled up in front of her house.

"The moon's full. The night sky is so bright out here."

"No city lights." She shot him a provocative look. "I guess I'd better get busy."

"Doing what?" he asked as they walked up the porch steps.

"Gathering herbs, of course."

"Ah, yes, for your herbal remedies. Don't you have to be naked?"

"Naturally," she said, flicking him a disdainful glance.

"Want some help?" he asked her, his smile slow and easy.

Her lips twitched. "An amateur would only get in the way. Besides, I can't do it before midnight."

Naked. Midnight. Talk about potent images, he thought. "I'm a quick study. And I don't have to leave."

"I was joking," she said.

"But I wasn't." He took a step closer to her.

Piper retreated against the door. Smiling, he edged closer still. "Piper," he said softly, "aren't you going to ask me in?"

She shook her head. "I don't think so."

The husky, whiskey sound of her voice gripped him. "Your grandfather's here."

"Yes." She ran her tongue across her lips.

The nervous gesture made the need to taste her irresistible. "Okay," he said, and drew her against him. He lowered his mouth to hers and slid into the kind of kiss he'd been thinking about since he'd met her. It was even better than he'd imagined, her soft, sexy mouth parting to admit him and her arms clutching around his neck. Then she flicked her tongue across his lips and slipped it inside his mouth.

He pulled her closer, tracing a hand down her supple curves. As the kiss lengthened he forgot everything. Forgot that he was supposed to be moving slowly, forgot that vulnerable look he'd seen in her eyes, forgot they were standing on her porch because she was too wary of him to let him come inside. Desire blasted through him, his body hardened, ached. His hand moved up to caress her breast, cupping it, the weight of it molding to his palm, the nipple already stiffening.

She moaned and wrapped her arms more tightly around his neck, pressing her breast into his hand. His other hand found the bare skin of her back and stroked it gently while he deepened the kiss in a journey toward pure explosion.

The sound of his beeper rent the quiet of the night, loud and grating. Piper jumped and tried to pull away from him. His hands slid to her waist and he slowly lifted his mouth from hers, staring at her while his beeper continued sounding. Muttering a foul word, he jammed a finger on the button.

Blessed silence. He leaned his forehead against hers and said, "May I use your phone?"

"My—" She stared at him blankly. "My phone?"

Releasing her took training, and a lot of willpower. "My pager. I need to phone the answering service."

"Oh. Oh, of course."

It wasn't the way he'd wanted to end the night.

Although she spent the next day up to her elbows in an herb mixture she decided Elizabeth Arden would kill to get, Piper couldn't help reliving the night before in her mind. Thank God Eric's beeper had gone off when it did. But had it saved her from committing a really stupid act or merely postponed the inevitable?

If she wanted to have an affair with Eric there was

nothing to stop her. Nothing except her disastrous past experience and the uncomfortable feeling that she wasn't cut out for affairs.

Chemistry. Sex. That's all it was. She wasn't an idealistic nineteen-year-old anymore, who thought that love was the answer and believed everything a man told her. No, she was a lot older and wiser, thanks to Dr. Roger Griffin. Cole's father.

Older and wiser, perhaps, but until she'd met Eric she hadn't realized the power that chemistry exerted. The phone shrilled insistently. "Pay the Piper," she answered.

"Charlie's hurt," Sam said bluntly. "Bring the truck down to the corral." The foreman sounded worried, an emotion Piper hadn't realized he possessed.

"What happened? How bad is it?"

"Just get here quick. And get that new doc out here. It's pretty bad to be takin' him all the way to Alpine."

"The hospital? Oh, my God, I'll be right there." She raced out of the greenhouse, envisioning all the horrible possibilities. Earlier that summer Charlie had been diagnosed with hypertension and had suffered a mild attack of angina. Was it his heart again?

Piper knew CPR, but Sam didn't, and as she climbed into the pickup, she again cursed the old man's stubbornness. His comment about CPR was so typical of the cowboy that even though he'd infuriated her, she'd had to smile.

"Now Piper," he'd drawled, the wrinkled leather of his face creasing with laughter. "I ain't never kissed a man before and I ain't intendin' to start now. Charlie's got a problem with his ticker and I'll call a doctor or take him to town, but I'm damned if I'm a gonna kiss it and make it well."

No argument of Piper's had swayed him and Charlie had backed him up.

She reached the corral, but what she saw bore no resemblance to the scene she'd imagined. Blood. That was her first and overwhelming impression. She climbed over the fence and fell on her knees beside her grandfather, lying on his back in the dusty corral. "What happened?"

"Damned new stallion," Sam answered, standing over her and Charlie. "I done told Charlie he had a mean streak a mile wide." Sam turned to shout at the man wrestling with the big horse. "Put the son of a bitch in the stall, but watch those hooves."

"Grandpa! Grandpa, can you hear me?"

Charlie peeled back an eyelid and glared at her. " 'Course I can hear you, girl. Think I'm deaf?"

Relief swept over her. "Oh, Lord, Grandpa, I could kill you for scaring me like this."

He winced and groaned. "Can't seem to get my breath. Damn, I knew better than to let him catch me like that."

Piper looked at Sam. The old man shrugged. "Two rear hooves, straight to the chest."

"Wonderful. I'll call Eric. Sam, what is that he's holding over those cuts?"

"George's shirt. Only thing we could find and he was bleedin' like a stuck pig. I said we shouldn'ta shod that horse with—"

"Shut up, Sam," Charlie said. "I'm in no shape to argue with you."

Sam grinned. "Mebbe this way I'll win one."

Piper left them to it, heartened by the exchange. If Charlie was squabbling with Sam, he must not be hurt as badly as he looked.

"Doctor's office," Eric's receptionist drawled.

"Effie Lou, it's Piper. Let me speak to the doctor."

"Brad was just asking about you the other day. We haven't seen you in a month of—"

Knowing from experience that Effie Lou would talk for half an hour, Piper cut her off. "I've got to talk to Eric. Grandpa's hurt."

"Right away," she said, suddenly professional.

Shortly Eric came on the line. "What's wrong, Piper?"

"My grandfather's been kicked by a stallion. In the chest. He's bleeding but we're applying pressure." She had to stop and take a deep breath. "Should I bring him to you or to the hospital in Alpine?"

"Is he conscious?"

"Yes." Glancing at her grandfather, she caught his scowl.

"Any other obvious problems?"

"He says he's having a hard time breathing." She turned her back to Charlie and lowered her voice. "He's got a heart condition."

"Do you know CPR?" Eric asked her.

"Yes."

"Good. Keep an eye on him and bring him in. I'll be here."

"Fifteen minutes, tops," Piper said.

Eric met them at the door to his clinic. He and Sam helped Charlie up onto the table in the exam room. "Thanks," Eric said. "I can handle it now. Piper, you can wait outside and I'll call you when we're finished."

She crossed her arms over her chest. "I'm not going anywhere. I've seen blood before."

"Dang it, Piper, do like he says," Charlie told her. "It's just a scratch."

"I'm not leaving," she said, glaring at them both and determined they wouldn't get rid of her.

"She's always been a stubborn little filly," Charlie said. "Might as well let her stay."

The examination took forever. Piper had to dig her nails into the palms of her hands to stop herself from screaming.

Finally, Eric said, "Mr. Stevenson, you need stitches in your chest and X rays, but I think you've got at least one broken rib. Piper says you have a heart condition, so you should have an EKG run to be safe. Is your regular doctor in Alpine? I can patch you up enough to get there."

"Not him. You do it."

"But Grandpa, what about your heart?"

"Heart, schmart. Get on with it, Doc," Charlie said, holding a hand to his chest. "Doesn't have a damn thing to do with my heart. I've broken ribs before."

"But, Grandpa—"

"Piper," Eric said, "he shows no overt signs of heart trouble. And I can run an EKG on him here. Let's fix him up and he can see his cardiologist later on." Turning back to Charlie, he said, "Lie down, Mr. Stevenson, so I can sew you up without leaving too big a scar." He punched the intercom. "Effie, I need your help in here."

Effie entered a few minutes later. As she started filling syringes, Piper decided they could handle the rest without her. "I think I'll go talk to Sam. Okay, Grandpa?"

Charlie grunted. Eric sent her a reassuring smile. "Have a cup of coffee. We'll be about an hour."

With a last glance at her grandfather, she walked out. In the waiting room she dropped into a chair and burst into tears.

"Piper? Ain't Charlie gonna be okay?" Sam asked.

"Eric thinks he'll be fine." She sobbed even louder.

"Women," Sam muttered in disgust, scratching his head. "Never make a blame bit of sense."

FIVE

Eric held up the X ray for Charlie and pointed. "You can see it plainly, even without the lightbox. Two cracked ribs, Mr. Stevenson."

"Call me Charlie, everybody does. Huh. So that's what a busted rib looks like."

Eric nodded. "All I can do for you is give you pain pills and tell you to take it easy." Which, if he knew anything about stubborn old ranchers, Charlie wasn't about to do.

"Don't like pain pills. And Sam can't manage alone."

Eric studied him for a minute and added, "You really should let your own doctor check you out."

The old man shook his head. "Nope, I want you to take care of me. Never liked that fella anyway."

"You might not like me, either," Eric said, grinning. "I'm going to tell Piper that you need to take it easy."

"Aw, Doc, don't do that. She'll fuss over me till I go crazy." Eric laughed, and a crafty light appeared in Charlie's eyes. "Say, Doc, I could put in a good word for you with her."

"No deal, Charlie."

Piper peered around the edge of the door. "Is he okay?"

"He'll do, if he gets some rest. Come on in. His heart's fine, the EKG shows no changes."

"Thank God. Eric, could I talk to you before we go?"

"Sure. Here, Charlie, let me help you down."

Although he tried to hide his pain, Charlie couldn't stop a groan as he slid off the table. He shot Piper a stern glance. "Don't be long, girl. Sam needs to get back."

"Is he really all right?" she asked Eric when her grandfather had gone.

"He'll hurt like hell because he's too stubborn to take the pain pills, but he'll be fine." Her head was bent, she wouldn't look at him. "Piper? He's going to be fine." Eric laid a comforting hand on her shoulder.

"It scared me," she said tightly. "When Grandpa had that angina earlier this summer, I realized he's not going to be around forever. Then, when Sam called me today, I—I thought he'd had a heart attack." Her blue eyes glistening with unshed tears, she looked up at Eric. "You probably think I'm a fool, that I'm overreacting."

"No, of course I don't." He patted her back soothingly. "It could have been much worse, enough to frighten anyone."

"But you said he was fine and now I'm—" She sniffled. "Crying like an idiot."

"It's perfectly normal to react this way."

For a moment she stayed silent, then she sniffled

again. "Thanks." She wiped her tears away with the backs of her hands, which made him smile.

"Anytime." His hand lingered on her shoulder. Though she looked better, her eyes were still anxious. She swayed toward him slightly. Suddenly comfort was the last thing on his mind. All he could think of was what it had been like when he'd kissed her the night before. And what it would be like when he kissed her again.

With static-filled tones, the intercom postponed whatever he might have done. "Dr. Chambers, your next appointment's here."

"Typical," he muttered. "Be right there, Effie." Regretfully, he dropped his hand. "Better now?"

A nod. "Yes. Well, I'll let you get to work."

"Have Charlie make an appointment with Effie in a week to remove the stitches. See you later."

"All right. Eric?"

He waited, his hand on the doorknob.

"Thank you. If I'd had to go to Alpine . . ."

"He would have been fine, Piper. But I'm glad I was here." Tempted to cancel his next appointment, he forced himself to leave.

It took her a day to work up the courage, but Piper asked Eric to dinner. As a thank-you for caring for Charlie, she assured herself. It had nothing to do with wanting to see him again. She was simply being polite.

She made lasagna. The layered, mouth-wateringly rich beauty of it always charmed her, enough so that even though it was time-consuming to assemble, she liked making it. It was perfect, every calorie-laden inch of it waiting to be savored, indulged in, rolled over the tongue like a fine wine.

The phone rang just as she finished, and she tracked the portable receiver to the bookshelf in the living room, sandwiched between the latest mystery best-seller and a book detailing organic pesticides. After hanging up, she absently set the phone down on the top of the TV and walked back to the kitchen. Horrified, she stared at the sight before her. Jumbo, his gargantuan paws planted firmly on the drainboard, was slurping up her prizewinning lasagna with tail-wagging enthusiasm.

"Jumbo, get down!" Grabbing a roll of paper towels, she whacked him on the head with it. Jumbo's bushy tail brushed against her leg as he buried his snout more deeply into doggie nirvana. "Miserable mongrel!" She jerked on his collar with one hand and rained paper blows on his rocklike head with the other. Jumbo looked up and belched.

"Oh, my beautiful lasagna." She moaned, almost in tears. Then she wrenched the dish out from under Jumbo's rampaging mouth and threw it in the sink.

Tongue lolling, his snout covered in tomato sauce and cheese, the dog regarded her hopefully. "You should at least have the decency to look contrite," she said as she threw him outside. He stood at the back door and barked loudly.

Hurriedly she set about making another casserole, but everything that went right with the first one went wrong with the second. Assembled, it looked like dog food hash, but it would have to do. The important thing was that it tasted good, she comforted herself. At four-thirty, she covered it with plastic wrap, slid it into the refrigerator, and left to salvage what she could out of the potting schedule she'd abandoned that morning.

Two hours later she rushed into the house, having forgotten that the clock in the greenhouse was broken. Eric was due in half an hour. "Grandpa," she shouted on her way through the living room, where Charlie sat watching TV, "put the lasagna in the oven for me. I'm late."

"Now, Piper, you know I can't cook worth a durn."

"Three seventy-five. Just pop it in, okay?"

No shirts, dammit. Why hadn't she ironed yesterday? Naked and dripping, she stood in front of her closet and wished she dared wear a dress, but Charlie would never let her hear the end of it and Cole was likely to ask her why she was so dressed up. It was enough of a novelty that she'd invited a man to dinner.

When the doorbell rang at precisely seven, Piper plastered a smile on her face, rubbed damp palms over her shorts, and swung open the door. Her words of greeting died on her lips. Eric wore a pair of stonewashed jeans and a crisp blue and white seersucker shirt sporting two huge, muddy pawprints on either side of his chest. One knee of his jeans was muddy, indicating he'd tried to protect himself with no success. Considering he was irritated as the dickens, she thought he looked quite handsome.

"Oh, Eric, I'm sorry," she said, trying not to laugh. "Jumbo's on my list too."

His look of irritation vanished in a reluctant grin. "It'll wash." He handed her a bottle of wine. "I hope red's okay. You didn't tell me what we were having."

The evening continued as it had begun. When they

sat down to eat, Cole pulled his routine of not wanting his dinner. Once Piper tasted the lasagna, she couldn't blame him. The only seasoning she'd remembered was the salt—and she'd remembered at least two or three times.

"Ooh, gross. What is this?" Cole asked, tearing away a clear stringy substance from the top of the casserole.

Piper stared at it and turned to glare at Charlie. "Didn't you take the plastic wrap off before you put it in the oven?"

Eric choked.

"Nope. You didn't tell me to," Charlie said with relish. "I *told* you I couldn't cook."

"Oh for—That's not cooking, it's common sense. Everyone knows to take the plastic wrap off before you cook it."

"I didn't."

The smug smile on his face made her want to bop him.

Without a tremor in his voice, Eric said, "We can just scrape it aside, Piper. It's not a problem."

She transferred her gaze to him. Ordinarily she had a good sense of humor. Ordinarily she'd have found this funny. Tonight she found the whole race of men a pain in the behind. That damned dog was male too. "Dessert is ice cream," she said, daring any of them to say a word. "Store-bought."

"Yum, ice cream," Cole said, happy at last.

After a rousing video game, Piper dragged Cole off to bed, leaving her grandfather to entertain Eric. When she came back, both of them were sound asleep, Charlie in his easy chair and Eric on the couch. She woke her grandfather and he went to bed.

A smile hovering on her mouth, Piper walked to the couch. Now there's an ego booster, she thought. Invite a man to dinner and he falls asleep halfway through the evening. Studying him, she decided he wasn't to-die-for good-looking. Not that he was ugly. Far from it. Sleep, however, hid some things about him. Such as his eyes, undoubtedly one of his best features. They changed with his mood, reminding her of the color of African violet leaves when they were gray and jade plants when they were green. Very expressive and, she thought ruefully, not a little seductive. His face was lean and even-featured, rather like his personality. His even temperament held a reassuring appeal. But his jaw—that was square, strong, and unless she was terribly mistaken, stubborn.

Even though he was tall and lanky, his shoulders were broad, and his chest was surprisingly hard, she remembered. With a lot more muscle than was readily apparent. She knew exactly when she'd become aware of that too. The first time he'd held her against him and kissed her, that's when.

Stop it, she told herself. *You're standing here practically salivating over the man while he's asleep, like a Venus flytrap lying in wait for the fly.*

"Eric." She put a hand on his shoulder and shook him gently. He didn't move a muscle. "Wake up." She shook harder. He turned his head against the cushion and mumbled something. Her hand poised to try again, she thought about how tired he'd looked earlier. Sighing, she went to find a blanket.

Three hours later, in her quest for a sleeping aid, Piper tiptoed into the kitchen for a glass of milk. Walking back through the living room, she almost jumped out of her skin when she heard Eric call her name. "You scared me to death," she said softly, walking over to the couch. "I thought you were asleep. I didn't mean to wake you." In the light thrown by the moon streaming into the window she could see his smile.

"I didn't mean to fall asleep."

"Do you do this often?" she asked him, grinning.

"Only when I haven't slept in three days. It's a talent, being able to fall asleep anywhere. During my residency I used to do it all the time." He yawned. "My ex-wife hated it."

"What's she like?" Piper asked, before she thought.

"Dawn?" He considered that a minute. "Beautiful," he said slowly. "Un—" He halted and shook his head.

If he hadn't been half-asleep, Piper imagined, he probably would have dodged that question entirely. She wondered what he'd been about to say, but it was plain he didn't want to talk about his marriage. "Why haven't you slept?"

He patted the couch beside him. "Why don't you have a seat and share some of that milk?"

Not a good idea, she thought, eyeing his form stretched out along the length of the sofa. She sat anyway, assuring herself she could handle whatever feelings he provoked. "Help yourself," she said, handing him the glass.

"First, my sister had twins." He took a deep drink of the milk. "I flew out to Dallas a few days ago to see them. Dr. Forrest could only cover me for a day, and when I returned I had a baby to deliver and an older lady who thought she'd broken her hip." After another drink he handed her back the milk.

"Gee thanks," she said, looking at the nearly empty glass. "Billie Mae Stubblefield had her baby?"

"How did you know? Oh, never mind. I forgot about small towns. Yeah, a boy."

"And the broken hip was Laura Simmons, right?"

"Not broken. But it took all night in the Alpine hospital to figure that out."

Piper set the glass down on the coffee table. "I guess I'd better go to bed."

"And I should leave, since I'm awake. Speaking of which, why didn't you wake me up and kick me out earlier?"

"You've got to be kidding. You sleep like the dead."

"Sorry," he said. He didn't look sorry, he looked . . . Oh, Lord, he looked like he was going to kiss her. His hand slid into her hair and he let it tangle over his fingers. "Such beautiful hair," he murmured. Her hair trailed over his arm and he rubbed his thumb across her lower lip.

Her blood began a slow heat, a simmer toward boiling. She tried to catch her breath, but couldn't.

"Do you want me to go?" he asked her.

"You probably should." The words came out in a whisper.

"But I asked if you wanted me to."

He held her gaze. She wished she were a young, carefree, innocent girl again. That she didn't know what could happen when she got caught up in her emotions. But she was a woman now, with needs long denied, sitting in the moonlight with a man she found much too attractive for her own good. "No," she finally said. "I don't want you to leave."

He exerted pressure on the back of her neck until her lips hovered within inches of his. "Kiss me good night, Piper."

She couldn't. She could only stare mutely and wonder where her good sense had fled to.

"Then I'll have to kiss you," he said. His lips pressed against hers and his tongue slid inside her mouth, parting her lips with a gentle pressure. She tasted temptation, exquisite temptation, a temptation that washed away her fears in an explosion of feeling. Helpless, her tongue met his in an erotic dance of pure pleasure while his hands fell to the lapels of her robe, hesitating a moment before he parted the material and touched her breasts.

With a hiss of indrawn breath she drew away and stared at him while he massaged her breasts, flicking the nipples with his thumbs until they stood in rigid peaks against the fabric of her thin nightshirt. Her blood pounded, an erratic rhythm of desire. "Eric," she said in a strangled whisper.

"Shh." He raised a hand to bring her mouth back down to meld with his, kissing her deeply, a slow, sweet, dizzying torture of the senses. His kisses, his hands kneading her breasts, his fingers teasing the nipples made her ache, made her want to forget everything except how wonderful what he was doing to her felt.

She was out of her depth and she knew it. This had to stop, now, before it went any further. She couldn't take the risk again, not again. Placing her hands against his chest, she pushed at him. "Eric, this isn't—we can't—"

He took one of her hands from against his chest. Slowly, so slowly, he turned it over and kissed her wrist, then her palm, all the while watching her eyes. "Why can't we?"

"Because I—because you—" Dammit, she felt like a teenager again. When his tongue stroked her palm, she almost forgot what she was saying. "I don't have casual sex." There, she'd finally managed a coherent sentence.

Bathed in the moonlight, his face suddenly looked harsher, almost angry. "Neither do I." He kissed her wrist again and her pulse throbbed erratically.

Remember what happened the last time you trusted a man, she told herself. "I'm not ready to take this step."

"Then we'll wait until you are."

"I'm not sure I ever will be."

He grinned. "You think not?" His gaze traveled from her face to her chest, where, she was achingly aware, the state of her arousal was still obvious. As he regarded her, his shoulders started to shake.

She bristled. "What's so funny?"

"You're the only woman I know who can make a Garfield nightshirt look sexy."

Her chin lifted. "My son gave me this shirt."

"Like I said, on you it looks great." He drew the lapels of her robe together over her chest, pulling her closer. His hands rested lightly at the valley of her breasts; their lips were a scant inch apart. "You're kidding yourself, you know." He pressed a quick, hot kiss on her lips and let go.

Piper flushed and jumped up from the couch. Someday she'd pay him back for all that arrogant male pride. "Don't count on it, buster."

Smiling, he rose from the couch and walked to the door. "It's damned near impossible not to, Angel. Thanks for dinner."

"Don't let the door hit you in the fanny on your way out."

Piper heard Cole's voice coming through the open greenhouse window. "Mom! Come see what I found!"

At least he'd waited until she was almost finished, Piper thought, slicing through the orchid cutting she was propagating. "Be there in a minute," she called to him, wondering what he wanted. Last time she'd heard that note of excitement in his voice he'd found a rattlesn—

Piper threw down her tools and rushed outside, her heart beating triple time. "Cole, you didn't—"

"Come on, Mom. Mirabelle had her kittens in the barn." He tugged on her hand, rushing her along at top speed.

Kittens, she thought, her heart rate settling. She could handle those a lot better than a nest of rattlers. In a corner of the barn, Mirabelle was purring over her litter of five kittens. The kittens couldn't be more than a couple of days old, Piper judged. She didn't bother cautioning Cole against touching them. Having lived on the ranch his entire life, he knew the rules.

"Why don't horses have as many babies as cats do?" Cole asked her as they watched the kittens nurse.

"That's just the way they're made, I guess," Piper

said. Unless he was in school, Cole was present at every birth on the ranch. He also dogged the vet's footsteps whenever he had occasion to come out. Not for the first time, Piper wondered if Cole would be a veterinarian when he grew up. She had mixed feelings about that, since she knew that big-animal vets had a hard time earning a living. But Cole was only six, so she wasn't too concerned yet.

Thoughts of vets led to thoughts of doctors. Or maybe that was because almost everything had her thinking about doctors lately. One particular doctor, anyway. Eric hadn't called her since he'd come to dinner, but it had only been two days. "Want to play catch?" she asked Cole in an effort to get her mind on the important things in her life. The things that mattered, not this fleeting physical attraction she felt for Eric Chambers.

"Cool," Cole said.

Cole looked like his father, she supposed, though by now Roger's image had faded and she had trouble recalling his exact features. Roger. Lord, how easy he'd found it to seduce her, even though she'd been engaged to Neil when they met. He'd swept aside her objections, and she had broken it off with Neil and tumbled into his arms. It didn't matter that she hadn't known Roger was married. She hadn't wanted to know, hadn't even considered all the signs that pointed to the truth. Piper would never again make the mistake of believing a man too easily.

"Will you pitch me some too?" Cole asked her, slipping a grubby hand in hers.

A week's worth of work awaited her in the greenhouse. Piper looked at her son and felt love squeeze her heart. "Sure," she said. "Let's go get the bat and gloves." Work could wait. Six-year-olds couldn't.

Forty-five minutes later she rushed into the greenhouse to find Eric there, wandering through the section devoted to her herbs. Her heart leaped at the sight of him, irritating her immensely. "What are you doing here?"

He smiled when he turned to look at her. She wished his smile didn't make her stomach knot with a fluttery, goofy feeling. "I thought the place was deserted," he said. "You weren't in the house or out here."

"I was at the barn. What do you want?" She knew she sounded ungracious, but she decided it was better that way.

"I know you've probably been to the McDonald Observatory, but I wondered if you and Cole wanted to go again. I'd like to see it."

Sneaky of him to include her son, she thought. "Sorry, I've got work. Seems like you should too. Don't you ever work?"

"Had a slow day." He studied her thoughtfully, then walked over to her.

Piper backed against the potting bench. "What?" she asked, when he raised his hand to brush his fingers across her cheek.

"Mud," he said, smiling as he wiped it away. "Are you sure you can't go?"

Be direct, she told herself. "This isn't going to work. I told you that the other night. I'm not having an affair with you."

"Why not?"

Well, that was blunt. She cast around for something,

anything to say. "I'm not interested. At least, not enough to go to bed with you."

"Are you saying you're not attracted to me?"

"Yes," she said, wishing he'd drop it and knowing he wouldn't.

"What about the other night? You seemed"—his gaze ran down her body before returning to her eyes—"interested then."

"Heat of the moment," she said, shrugging. "It was late, we were half-asleep."

He stepped even closer, taking hold of her arms. "Neither of us is half-asleep now. Are we?"

Her blood heated, her mind turned to mush as she felt the current of heat flow between them. "N-no. What are you doing?"

He pulled her against him and crushed his lips to hers in a kiss that literally knocked her senseless. She curled her fingers into the hair at his nape. Hunger. Heat. From him, and worse, from herself as his tongue swept through her mouth. Not sweet, or gentle, or even seductive, but explosive energy and hot desire. In one sweeping, arousing motion, he ran his hands deliberately down her body. When she was nothing but a quivering pool of sensation, he finally stopped. Her eyes opened to see the anger in his gaze.

"I'd say that proved you a liar, Angel. What do you say?"

He was breathing a little heavily, but that was his sole reaction to a kiss that had robbed her mind of any sane thought and her body of its will. "I'd say it makes you a jackass."

"Probably." He bent his head to kiss her again, but she placed a hand on his chest.

"Don't. Please."

Their gazes locked and held. Eric released her and stepped back, raking his hands through his hair and muttering a curse.

After a long, awkward silence, Piper spoke. "You probably think it's strange that a woman like me would hesitate about something like this."

He shot her a puzzled glance. "What's that supposed to mean? 'A woman like you'?"

"Well . . ." She lifted her shoulders. "There's Cole. Don't pretend you haven't heard that he's illegitimate." God, she hated that word. Such a cruel word for an innocent little boy.

"So? Are you saying that because you have an illegitimate son, I believe that entitles me to take you to bed?"

She winced and turned her head. "You wouldn't be the first."

He swore, crude, succinct, and to the point. "Dammit, look at me." She forced herself to meet his gaze. "That kiss just now was about my ego. Because you said you weren't attracted to me, not because you said you wouldn't sleep with me. Good God, do you think I'm so hard up I have to con a woman into bed?"

She smiled. "No, I think you might have to fight them off, if you kissed them like you kissed me."

He paced away and then back, glaring at her. "Do you think—" he continued furiously, then stopped. "What?"

"You heard me. Do you have to fight women off?"

A reluctant smile stole over his face. "Not anytime

lately. And I haven't had to fight you off at all." He took her hand. "Nothing will happen until you're ready for it."

"What if I never am?"

His fingers gentle, he stroked her face. She found it oddly soothing. "Just what kind of men have you been dating, Piper?"

"The wrong kind, obviously."

He gave her cheek a last caress and dropped his hand. "Why don't you let me worry about what I'll do, if and when? You just worry about what you really want to do."

But what she wanted to do and the smart thing for her to do were two entirely different matters.

SIX

Over the next week, Piper, Cole, and Eric took in more sights than she'd realized existed in the area. Finally, tired of her constant chaperon, Piper asked Lynn to take care of Cole the next time she went out with Eric.

Eric didn't treat her any differently, though. While she appreciated the lack of pressure, she wondered if he now thought of her more as a sister than a potential lover. She loathed feeling like a sister. What was wrong with her? One minute she told him to wait, because she wasn't ready. Then when he did what she asked, she couldn't stand it. She was hopeless.

"It's early," he said, opening her car door after another trip to McDonald Observatory. "Do you want to pick up a movie?"

"Okay. But we'll have to watch it at your place, our VCR is acting up."

"My place?" He sounded uneasy.

"You know, Eric, if I didn't know better, I'd think you were hiding something from me. You've never let me see your apartment."

"I didn't know you wanted to. It's just an apartment."

"Which you don't want me to see."

He glanced at her, looking baffled. "If it's that important to you, why didn't you say so before?"

"All I'm saying is, it seems a little odd that you've never taken me there." The more she thought about it, the angrier she grew. Was he hiding something? She'd made the mistake of believing too easily before.

"There's nothing at all odd about it."

He sounded exasperated and that made her even angrier. "So you admit you've been avoiding taking me to your place?"

He pulled off the road into one of the roadside stops. "Hell yes, I admit it. What do you think is going to happen if you and I are alone together at my place?"

"Absolutely nothing, if the last week is anything to go by," she said, stung into blurting out another concern.

He gripped her arms and his mouth came down on hers, hard, hot, and not at all brotherly. Shocked, she opened to the invasion and moaned, sliding her arms around his neck. With rhythmic persuasion, his tongue thrust and withdrew, meeting hers, teasing her, tempting her.

Against her lips, he spoke roughly. "Trying to keep my hands off you has been driving me nuts."

"I thought you didn't want—" She gasped, realizing he'd undone her blouse. Her bra clasp gave way and he spread the material open, staring at her bare breasts. Her heart beat faster as her nipples hardened and responded to his intent gaze.

His lips trailed down her neck, tracing a heated path. When he reached the peak of her breast, he drew the aching tip into his mouth and closed his lips around it. Her blood ran hotter still while he suckled her breast, the heat and the feel of his lips and tongue pushing her to a reckless desire. Lost in pleasure, she arched her back and felt one of his hands slide down to the juncture of her thighs. It felt so good. Too good. He handled her like a master and she blossomed under the expert care. No, she couldn't, she wouldn't. She put her hands against his chest and pushed.

He drew back, looking at her while his hand continued fondling her breast. She knew he wasn't unaffected. His heavy breaths and the hard line of his jaw told her, as well as the certainty that if she let her glance fall to his lap, she'd see unmistakable evidence of his arousal.

"That's why I haven't taken you to my place," he said. "Much more of this and you'll be on your back with me inside you."

His blunt words sent a thrill through her, but though she wanted to, she couldn't permit herself to respond.

"You're still not ready, are you?"

"I'm sorry," she said in a choked voice. "You must think—"

"Shh." He covered her mouth with his fingers. "When we make love I don't want there to be any regrets."

No regrets. Piper wondered if that were possible. He kissed her again, then started the car while she rearranged her clothes.

"You can come over tomorrow night," he said. "But bring Cole with you."

Ashamed of doubting him, she nodded. If only she'd been as suspicious with Roger. But if she had, she wouldn't have Cole.

Another sleepless night. Eric swore, got out of bed, and walked over to the window. Leaning against the sill, he had a momentary wish that he could get drunk. Tonight he was covering for Steve Forrest, so that option was out. He wasn't much for drinking anyway. Dammit, the only times he ever had insomnia were when he was worried about a patient. Otherwise he slept, even during the worst crisis. So what was he doing, pacing his bedroom at three o'clock in the morning? Again.

Losing his mind from sexual frustration, that's what. He wanted to make love to Piper so badly, he was flat losing it. And she wasn't ready. That was abundantly clear. Maybe he wasn't either. He laughed at that thought. Physically, sure. But mentally . . . This wasn't about rational thought processes, though. It was about a basic need that he'd left unsatisfied for quite a while.

Simply because he liked Piper, respected her, enjoyed being with her didn't mean he'd fall in love with her. Or want to marry her, God forbid. One failed marriage was plenty. Eric wasn't a man who took failure well. No, the problem was that he didn't want to hurt Piper. She wanted to be with him, but she was afraid. How could he convince her that she wouldn't be hurt when he couldn't possibly guarantee that?

He slapped his hand against the window frame and groaned. No relief in sight, he thought. Effie was probably ready to take a contract out on him, he'd been so hard to get along with lately. Frustration was close to killing him. He knew the remedy for what ailed him. Too bad it didn't look like he'd be cured anytime soon.

After he'd seen his last patient the next day, Eric didn't hesitate before driving to the Stevenson ranch. Standing at the door to Piper's greenhouse, he remembered the first time he'd seen her. Though he still had the same gut-punch reaction to her, he now knew there was much more to her than her gorgeous face and body. She was smart, courageous, and amazingly sweet. He shifted, uneasy again at his train of thought. Sexual desire was understandable, but liking her—that was far more dangerous. That could lead to serious things, and he wasn't ready for serious. He swung the door open and walked in. From the sounds he guessed she was at the potting bench in the back.

She was standing with her back to him. "You're late," she said without turning.

"Am I?"

Piper whirled, the large pot she held dropping from her hands and crashing on the gravel floor. Her hand clutched her chest. "Eric! You scared me to death. I thought you were Gus."

"No." He dug his hands into the pockets of his pants and leaned back against the bench. "Are you spraying again?" She wore a Mickey Mouse T-shirt and looked sexy as hell in it.

"Spraying? No." Silent for a moment, she gazed at him. "I wasn't expecting you."

"Do you want me to go?"

"No." Her tongue touched her top lip. "What did you want?"

You, he wanted to say. "To see you," he said instead. His stomach tightened. Nervously, she licked her lip again and his groin tightened too. "I can't sleep. Hell, I can hardly think. I want you so much it's driving me crazy."

Her eyes were huge, intensely blue, and fixed on his face. "I can't sleep, either," she said quietly.

"Why?"

"The same reason you can't."

In two strides, he closed the distance between them and took her in his arms, kissing her with barely re-strained violence. He felt her go pliant against him as she responded, kissing him back, her hands racing over his body, just as his did over hers.

"Eric, this is crazy," she said, her lips against his.

"No, this is good." He cupped her bottom and pulled her more tightly against him. Buried his head in the curve of her neck and smelled her fragrance. Ran his lips along the smooth line of her throat and heard the thud of her heart, her choppy breathing. He wanted to lay her down, right there among the flowers and plants, on the gravel floor of the greenhouse, and make love with her until he was finally sated, but he remembered that he was a civilized man. And she deserved much more than that. So he placed his hands on her waist and set her away from him.

"Tonight? You'll come to my place?" he asked hus-kily.

She looked as dazed as he felt. "When?"

Her lips were swollen from his kisses, her eyes wide,

the pupils dilated. "Seven?" He kissed her again. "Six-thirty." Again. Harder, longer. "Six." He stared at her for a moment and said, "To hell with it. Can you lock that door?"

She gave a shaky laugh. "I don't think I'd better."

"Are you sure about that?" One hand grazed her bottom, the other fit the small of her back and pulled her closer.

"Seven," she murmured, but she kept kissing him.

"Darling," an amused feminine voice said, "if I'd known you were involved with a man instead of those grubby little plants, I'd never have walked in. Definitely an improvement."

They turned to look at the woman standing a few feet away. Piper started to pull away, but Eric tightened his hold.

"Don't stare so, darling," the woman said. "Surely you recognize me. It hasn't been that long."

"Mother? What are you doing here?"

"Interrupting, obviously," she said, her voice rich with amusement. "Do introduce me. I've yet to meet the man who can take you away from your posies."

Eric stifled a groan. Piper frowned at him and turned around, again trying to pull free. He caught her shoulders, holding her in front of him. "Stay put," he muttered in her ear, and knew by the flush rising up her cheeks that she'd realized his dilemma.

Haltingly, Piper introduced them. The wicked laughter in her mother's eyes left no doubt that she understood his problem too. "Charmed to meet you, Mr. Chambers. And call me Kimberly."

"It's Dr. Chambers," Piper said.

"Eric," he said. While it was clear the two women were related, at first the differences between them were more apparent than the similarities. That might be due to the way they were dressed. Piper wore a T-shirt, cut-offs, neon green socks, and sneakers. Her mother wore a pale pink suit that screamed designer, complete with matching pumps and purse.

Kimberly's hair, pale blond and cut to shoulder length, was perfectly coifed, sprayed, and groomed. Her daughter's hung in a wild mass of curls to the middle of her back. Piper didn't suffer from the comparison, though. He much preferred her turbulent beauty to the ice-princess looks of her mother.

"Shall I go out and come back in?" Kimberly asked. "Or would you prefer that I just leave?"

Eric realized with a spurt of amusement that she'd been sizing him up too. "No need, I was leaving," he said, under control now. "I'll see you tonight, Piper. At six."

"Seven," she corrected him, not missing the look he gave her. She doubted her mother did either.

"Fascinating," Kimberly said to Piper after Eric left. "Your taste is improving. Deliciously sexy, don't you think?"

"Mother—"

"Of course you do," she said approvingly. "Oh, don't worry darling, I've sworn off men."

Piper snorted inelegantly. "I'm sure Leonardo would be devastated to hear that."

Her mother gave an airy wave of her hand. "A thing of the past."

No doubt, Piper thought. Kimberly changed men

nearly as often as other women changed underwear. Leonardo had lasted a record three months. "Why are you here?"

"To see you and my grandson, of course."

"Hiding again, Mother?"

She laughed, a musical tinkle. "Really darling, you could always read me so well. Leonardo thinks I've flown off with a new lover. Jealousy is so mundane, but sometimes there's nothing like it for getting a man's attention." She looked around the greenhouse and shuddered delicately. "Can we go inside before I positively melt from this humidity?"

"You go ahead. I've got to clean up this mess."

Kimberly turned to go, adding over her shoulder, "I want to hear all about this new man when you come in."

And wouldn't rest until she did, Piper thought, bending to pick up the broken pieces of clay.

A short time later Piper found her mother in the living room. Kimberly sat on the sofa sipping a glass of chilled white wine and observing her daughter for all the world, Piper thought, like she was about to conduct an interview with one of her models.

"I'd love to stay and chat," Piper said breezily, "but I have a date. Cole will be back soon. I'm sure he and Grandpa will be happy to see you."

"The day Charlie is happy to see me," her mother stated, "I'll be in a coffin."

Piper laughed, not contradicting her. Charlie wasn't a subtle man. "Cole always enjoys seeing you." Kimberly and Cole got along surprisingly well, considering Kimberly didn't have a maternal bone in her body.

"Tell me about your new man before you go."

"He's not my new man, he's a—a friend of mine."

"A friend?" Kimberly arched a delicate eyebrow. "My dear . . ."

"Mother, I'm not one of your models you can quiz at will. Why are you so interested?"

"Well, darling, I need something to do while I'm here. And to my knowledge you haven't been involved with a man since the regrettable Roger."

"What makes you think I'm involved now?" Nonchalantly, she hoped, Piper crossed her arms over her chest.

"Come now, I'm not blind. I am dreadfully curious why you decided to take the plunge again."

"What plunge?"

"Coming back to life, my dear. Sleeping Beauty?"

Piper's lips quirked but she managed not to laugh. "Wrong fairy tale. Sleeping Beauty wasn't twenty-seven with a child. And life isn't a fairy tale, in my experience."

"True enough," Kimberly agreed with a careless shrug. "Fine, if you won't talk, you won't. What are you wearing?"

"What I have on, if you don't let me go."

"I brought something for you. Perhaps you'll wear it tonight."

Piper's eyes softened. Although extremely self-centered, her mother could also be generous. "That's sweet of you, but we're not going anywhere fancy."

"Just a casual little number. I'll put it on the bed and you can see it after you've showered."

"Thank you." At the doorway Piper stopped and

looked over her shoulder. "It's good to see you, Mother."

With a dimpling of her cheeks that made her look amazingly like her daughter, Kimberly said, "Next time I'll try to make sure my entrance comes at a more opportune moment."

Her mother's idea of casual and Piper's were worlds apart, but Piper could no more resist the dress Kimberly had brought her than she could have a new species of orchid. An unusual shade of violet—the same color that tinged the inner petals of one of her orchids—the dress was soft, cool, and inviting, designed to tempt a man, with a snug scooped bodice, short, flouncy skirt, and a row of tiny buttons that ran from neckline to hem. Perfect, she thought.

What have I gotten myself into? Piper wondered an hour later, sitting ramrod straight on Eric's couch and trying not to hyperventilate.

"Would you like a drink?" he asked her.

"No—Yes. A glass of wine would be nice." Now that the time had come, she wanted to run. Why hadn't she told him she couldn't make it tonight? She wasn't ready. Would he kill her if she told him she'd changed her mind? She took the glass from him and drained half of it in a gulp. "Aren't you having any?"

A smile played at the corners of his mouth. "I'm not nervous," he said, taking a seat beside her. "Do you want me to take you home?" He toyed with her hair, then slid his hand up to her ear.

"No, of course not." Yes, she said silently, panicking.

His finger traced a path around her ear and down her neck. Wishing it didn't feel so seductive, she shivered. Eric took the wineglass from her nerveless fingers and set it on the table. He brought her hand to his mouth, kissed it, ran his thumb over the knuckles before he rose and drew her to her feet.

"What's wrong?" he murmured, pulling her close and nuzzling her ear. His hand stroked down her back, skimmed her hips. "Are you having second thoughts?"

And third and fourth, she thought. "No, nothing's wrong." *Stop analyzing everything to death, Piper*, she told herself. She wanted him, he wanted her. It should have been simple, but it wasn't.

Eric lifted a hand to her face, tracing her mouth with his finger. "Are you afraid?"

"Yes," she whispered.

"All you have to do is tell me no, Angel. That's all."

She believed him, trusted him that much, at least. Somehow, the knowledge freed her. "I don't want to say no."

"I want you, Piper." He slid his hands into her hair and tilted her head back so he could look deep into her eyes. "So much I think I'm losing my mind."

It was simple after all, she discovered. "Kiss me."

He bent to cover her mouth with his, gently at first but soon growing bolder. She opened to him as the kiss deepened, meeting his tongue with hers, locking her arms around his neck, abandoning herself to passion. His arms tightened around her, cradling her close as he ran his hands over her bottom, caressing her hips. Pressed against her, his hard flesh made her ache with wanting him. Again and again, he kissed her, withdrawing his tongue and thrusting back inside until she thought she could bear it no longer.

His hips rocked against her and he took her moans, her breathless sighs into his mouth as he kissed her. She couldn't remember feeling like this before, this wanting, this needing, this fever to feel her bare flesh against his.

Suddenly he bent and swung her up into his arms, striding from the room with her, his mouth never leaving hers. And then she was on her back in his bed, his hands at the buttons of her dress, stripping it from her rapidly. She reached for him and kissed him, running her hands over his chest, wondering if this was a dream she would wake from.

"I've wanted you for so long," he said. "You're even more beautiful than I imagined, like this, naked in my bed."

Deep and husky, his voice made her throb. Unsure what to say, she took his hand and placed it on her breast. He smiled, turning his hand over to graze her nipple with the back of it before bending to take her in his mouth once more.

Piper let her head fall back as his lips blazed a path down her throat and found the hammering pulse beating in its hollow. His thumbs teased the peaks of her breasts to tautness before he found her nipple with his tongue and she arched upward, desperate for more. He ran his lips, his tongue, from one damp crest to the other, leaving a scalding trail in the wake of his sensual assault.

Eric took her hand, placed it over his erection. "Feel what you do to me, Piper. That's how much I want you."

The words and the knowledge were seductive. Daring, she squeezed gently, and heard him suck in his breath. His fingers ran over her breast, down her stomach until he reached her thighs. "Careful, Angel, or this will be over sooner than I planned."

Ruthlessly he drove her up to the crest, until she shuddered, straining, quivering, arching as his hands and mouth played a reckless tune over her body. Seeking release, her hips bucked against his hand. He groaned and drew in a deep breath before he rolled away from her and jerked open the drawer of his bedside table. Dazed, she watched him rip open a foil packet. Hesitantly, she said his name, wanting him yet frightened by the intensity of her desires. He swept his hands down her thighs, parting them, then he entered her, and though she gave a choked-off cry, she didn't resist.

"Am I hurting you?" The words sounded forced and he began to draw back.

"No. Don't stop." The first pain of his intrusion had given way to a deeper ache, one that only he could assuage. She lifted her hips to his and whispered, "Don't stop, don't stop."

"I won't." With a sound that was part laugh, part groan, he said, "I can't." Sheathed inside her, he started the smooth, erotic rhythm, plunging in and out of her until she clamped her thighs tightly around his hips and felt him harden even more.

Sex wasn't supposed to be like this, she thought, had never been like this. His hand slid between them and he ran his fingers into the silky tangle of curls, searching . . . Her legs tightened around him and she went rigid, then crashed over the edge, hanging weightless as she came apart into a thousand pinpoints of pleasure.

He kissed her fiercely, plunging deeper and faster until she heard him cry out and she felt his pleasure in the last hard, lingering thrust, the shudder of satisfaction that rippled through his body.

SEVEN

"What are you thinking?" Eric asked Piper later, holding her in the curve of his arm. He could think now, just barely. And talk, just barely.

"I'm thinking"—she gave a catlike stretch—"that I feel wonderful."

Pleased with her answer, he smiled at her. "Is that a fact?"

"That's a fact. You have an amazingly smug expression on your face." She ran a fingertip down his cheek and smiled back.

"Who, me?" He kissed her jaw, then rolled over on top of her, propping himself on his forearms. "What would I have to be smug about?" He pressed a hot, greedy kiss to her lips. "Other than the fact that I've finally got you where I want you."

She lifted an eyebrow and looped her arms around his neck. "Oh, and where would that be?"

"In my bed." With his tongue, he traced an intricate pattern in the valley between her breasts. God, she was so responsive. Even though they had just finished making love, her reaction made him want her again.

"Hmm," she said, and shivered. "I have to admit"—he tasted the curve of her breast—"it's definitely a good place to be."

"Tell me something, Piper."

"Mmm. What?" She traced a finger over his lips and he turned his face into her palm and kissed it.

"That was the first time for you, wasn't it?"

Her breath caught. "Don't be silly, I have a son."

"There are other firsts." Slanting her a grin, he went back to nuzzling her breasts. His hand slipped down to the tangle of soft blond curls at the apex of her thighs. "That was your first climax." Captivated, he watched a flush spread over her skin.

"Why do you think that?"

"I don't think it, I know it." He slid upward and kissed her mouth, then pulled back to gaze into her eyes. "And you weren't expecting it," he said, dipping a finger inside her.

"Eric." Soft, breathless, she moaned his name.

Slowly, he withdrew, added another finger, and sank into her again. "I'm glad it was me." He knew a primitive and admittedly macho satisfaction that he had given her that first taste of mindless pleasure.

She moaned again and shifted her hips to match the rhythm of his hand. "I should probably go . . ." Her hand fell to the bed and clutched at the rumpled sheets.

Drawing her nipple into his mouth, he sucked on it strongly. "Not yet," he murmured. No, there was no way he'd let her go yet. He hadn't gotten nearly enough of her.

"But I thought we were . . ." Her voice trailed off as he subjected her other breast to the same treatment while his hand grew even more insistent.

"Thought we were what?"

"Oh!" She gripped his shoulders. "Aren't we finished?"

Raising his head from her breasts, he looked at her, watching her eyes darken with desire. "Just getting started, Angel," he said, and covered her mouth with his.

Eventually, he took her home. When he kissed her at her door, he realized he might have a serious problem. He wanted her again, as he had after the first time, and the second. How could he be completely satisfied after making love and then turn right around and want her again? Uneasily, he wondered if that feeling would fade with time and familiarity. It had to, didn't it?

"Darling," Kimberly said the next morning, "at least try to look a little less delirious." She shuddered. "It's indecent at seven o'clock in the morning."

"Mother, I didn't expect you to be up." Delirious. That was an apt description, Piper thought, and smiled.

Kimberly sipped her coffee, observing her shrewdly. "There's really no need to ask, it's written all over your face. You're in love with him. Ah, the wonders of love."

Her gaze flew to meet her mother's. "Don't be ridiculous. I'm"—her lips curved as she thought about it—"crazy about him. But I'm not in love."

Kimberly flicked her a smile. "I realize I haven't been a conventional mother, but you're still my daughter and I know you. You'd never have slept with him if you didn't love him."

Piper frowned. "Why are you so sure I slept with him?"

"Please," Kimberly said, and gave a dry laugh. "Give me some credit. I know a morning-after look when I see one. I ought to."

Piper rose and poured herself another cup of coffee. "Mother, I appreciate the interest, but I really don't think we need to go into this. If I did without your advice when I was a child, I can certainly do without it now."

"That's putting it bluntly, isn't it?" Kimberly said, her face going pale.

"I'm sorry." Though she tried not to, a part of her still resented her mother for not raising her. Sometimes it showed.

For a moment her mother looked sad. "All I meant to do was offer you an ear, if you needed it. However close you are to Charlie, he's not a woman."

Piper laughed, breaking the tension. "No, he's definitely male."

"Does Eric know about Cole?"

Piper picked up her coffee, warming her hands on the cup. "He knows he's illegitimate. I'm not sure what else he's heard."

"Will you tell him?"

Not unless she had to. "He hasn't asked and I haven't offered."

"If you're—" Kimberly hesitated and began again. "If you're serious about him, you might consider telling him yourself. Men have a nasty habit of finding out things we'd rather they didn't, and usually with the worst possible timing."

"I'm not ashamed of having Cole, Mother."

"But you are ashamed of what happened. Why you chose to shoulder all the blame is more than I can understand. You were only a child. He should have paid a heavier price."

"Nineteen isn't a child. It's old enough to know better." Had she really been that naive? How could she not have known that Roger was lying? Had lied from the time she met him until the last time she saw him, sitting in the courtroom at his wife's trial for attempted murder.

Piper could forgive herself for her naïveté, but she couldn't forgive herself for not *wanting* to know. She'd believed the lies because she had wanted the fairy tale to be true. When the truth had exploded in her face, she knew she'd been deliberately blind.

Just then Cole came in, demanding breakfast and a kiss, and the moment passed. But later, after taking her mother to the airport, Piper thought about what Kimberly had said. Her mother and grandfather still thought of her as the innocent girl who'd ruined her life by falling for the wrong man. Truth was, she hadn't been that girl for years. The barrage of publicity, the hounding from the press, being an unwed mother in a small Texas town, had destroyed any innocence she'd had left.

Because she had wanted a family—a normal family—so desperately, she'd been blind to the truth about Roger. She had that family now, though not the traditional one. But she had her son and she had no illusions. Cole was the important one.

Her relationship with Eric wouldn't last, but she had

gone into it knowing that full well. This time the blinders were off. If she didn't fall in love with Eric, then he lost the power to hurt her, whatever happened in the future. So she would enjoy what she had with him for as long as it lasted. And when it was over, she would walk away with her heart intact.

In the meantime, though, Eric was waiting for her. The night before, when he'd brought her home, he'd asked her to meet him in town for lunch. The thought of seeing him again sent a thrill coursing through her veins. Nothing to worry about, she assured herself. They'd just become lovers. She was supposed to feel this way.

Effie wasn't at her desk and no one answered when Piper called out. Thinking he hadn't heard her, she walked back to his office. The door was ajar, so she knocked and shoved it open.

Eric was leaning against his desk. A gorgeous redhead stood close beside him, talking earnestly. They looked up in surprise at Piper's entrance.

"Oh, I'm sorry," she said. "I didn't realize you were with a patient." Must have just moved here, Piper thought. She sure didn't look like she belonged in Capistrano.

"Don't go, Piper," Eric said, straightening. "Dawn was just leaving."

Dawn? Oh, Lord, *this* was his ex-wife? This walking advertisement for *Vogue*? The woman was stunning, a striking redhead flawlessly attired in an elegant powderblue suit. Piper felt slightly nauseated.

"Yes, don't go. I'm Dawn Chambers," the vision said, offering a hand.

"Piper Stevenson," Piper replied automatically.

Why, oh why had she worn her work clothes to town? At least her jeans and T-shirt weren't muddy, but compared to Dawn's perfection, she looked and felt like a total slob. Jealousy slashed through her like a hot knife through butter.

"Happy to meet you," Dawn said. Turning back to Eric, she added, "What about later? We could have a drink. Or dinner."

With a sinking feeling, Piper watched Eric.

He shook his head. "Piper and I have plans."

"I . . . see." Dawn gazed at him for a long moment before she finally said, "I'd better be going."

Piper almost felt sorry for her, except she was too busy being relieved that Eric hadn't taken his ex-wife up on her offer. And wondering why in the devil he'd divorced her in the first place.

"A pleasure meeting you," Dawn told Piper. She put her hand on Eric's arm. "It was good to see you again, Eric."

He didn't answer, or make a move to see her out. With a last, revealing look at him, she left. An awkward silence ensued until Piper broke it. "She's still in love with you."

He jammed his hands in his pockets and paced away from her. "No. She isn't."

"If you're thinking of getting back together with her—"

"That's the last thing that's going to happen," he said bitterly. "No matter what Dawn thinks. Don't worry about it."

Piper's temper spiked. "How can I help but worry about it? I walk in and find you with your ex-wife—your

gorgeous ex-wife who wants you back—and I'm not supposed to worry?"

Turning around, he frowned at her. "There's not a
chance in hell we'll get back together. God knows why
she bothered coming here. It's not enough that she—"
Abruptly, he broke off, his hands balled into fists. "Let's
just drop it."

Drop it? Oh, he'd like that, wouldn't he? "Just like
that? Forget about it because you said to? I don't think
so, Eric."

He took hold of her arms and said carefully, "I don't
want her back. This doesn't have anything to do with
you and me."

Didn't it? "But she—she was your wife. You were—"
Intimate with her, Piper thought, unable to continue the
sentence aloud. Dawn knew him in ways she might never
know him. Her stomach jolted unpleasantly. "You had a
life together. Memories. You must have some feelings
left for her."

He gave a harsh bark of laughter, released her, and
strode away from her. His back to her, he spoke. "Believe me, they're not the kind of feelings that would lead
me to marrying her again."

Or marrying anyone, Piper thought, though he
hadn't said the words. That was fine. She wasn't interested in marriage, either. But meeting his ex-wife had
shaken her, more than she'd ever imagined it would. She
wished—Oh, why did the woman have to be gorgeous?
And . . . nice, dammit. What could have made him so
bitter toward her? What had happened between them?

He wouldn't tell her unless she pushed him. Did she
have the right to do that? When she wasn't looking for

forever, either? Eric hadn't lied to her. That was the
important thing. She could deal with his ex-wife wanting
him back as long as he didn't want Dawn back. At least,
she hoped she could. "All right," she said. "It doesn't
matter."

Turning, he stared at her in surprise. After a long
moment he said, "You mean that, don't you? You won't
be angry if I don't tell you."

She crossed the room to lay a hand on his arm. "No,
I won't be angry."

For a minute he looked at her, his expression completely blank. When he spoke his voice was as expres-
sionless as his face. "She had an affair with a friend of
mine. I came home unexpectedly one day and found
them together."

She closed her eyes, opening them after a few seconds. "Oh, Eric. I'm sorry."

"We'd been having serious problems. That was
Dawn's way of dealing with them. I guess it shouldn't
have been such a surprise to me, but—" He broke off,
his eyes hard. "Call me old-fashioned, but I have a problem with adultery. Especially when my wife is committing it."

"I'm sorry," she said again, unsure what else to say.

"It happens." A shrug. "I've gotten over it."

No, he hadn't, she thought, but she knew he needed
to believe he had. Infidelity. Adultery. Oh, God, what
would he do when he found out the truth about her?

The next evening they attended an engagement party
for an old friend of Piper's.

"You make it real hard for me to drum up any interest in this party," Eric said when he picked her up. His gaze wandered over her slowly. "Are you sure you want to go?"

Piper laughed. "Marianne would shoot me if I didn't. I've known her forever."

Going to a party with a date for a change was fun, Piper decided, and it didn't hurt a bit that he was currently the area's most eligible bachelor. But every time she caught Eric's eye, he gave her a smile that made her blood race and her insides shaky. Somehow, she didn't think they'd stay long at the party.

Lynn strolled up and they exchanged greetings. "Thanks for taking care of Jason this afternoon," she told Eric.

"No problem. Jason's a good kid."

"How can you say that? He threatened to bite Effie Lou."

"Yeah, but he didn't try to bite me," he said, grinning, drawing a laugh from Lynn and Piper.

"What happened?" Piper asked.

"Three stitches and a tetanus shot," Lynn told her, shaking her head.

Lynn then proceeded to inform Piper, through a series of weird facial contortions, that she wanted to talk to Piper alone, so Piper sent Eric to get her a drink. When he left he gave her a look that suggested he knew she was trying to get rid of him. "Lynn," she said to her friend, "subtle you're not. Okay, what's up?"

"Neil's been holding forth about your lurid past."

"That's nothing new. He's drunk, I'm sure."

"As a skunk." Lynn nodded in agreement. "Slimy as

always. He's hitting on Marianne's little sister." She waved a hand in the direction of the pool. "Not that she minds."

Piper goggled at her. "Why in the world would she want him? Even Angela knows he'll never divorce Nadine."

"Who knows?" Lynn shrugged. "Myself, I'd rather do it with a snake, but there's no accounting for tastes."

Laughing, Piper agreed. "Thanks for the warning. I'll steer clear of him."

"You'd better steer Eric clear of him, too, unless you want his ears filled with garbage."

"Maybe I should tell him myself. If he finds out about Roger . . ." Her voice trailed off as she thought of what he'd said about Dawn.

"My God, honey, it was years ago. Why should he hear anything about it? Unless it's from Neil, of course."

"You know how people are." When she'd first returned from Lubbock, not everyone had been as understanding and supportive as Lynn. "Scandals, even old ones, never completely go away." Eric returned with her drink, and the three of them started talking about something else.

A little while later, when Marianne's mother had cornered Eric, Piper tried to find Marianne to tell her they were leaving. Pushing open the door to the music room, she found Neil instead. Before she could back out, he grabbed hold of her arm.

"Ah, the beautiful Piper Stevenson," he said, slurring the words. Slapping his free hand on the wall beside her face, he breathed whiskey fumes at her. "Any success with your latest victim? Has he found out you're a cheap little gold digger yet? 'Lolita of the West,' didn't the papers call you?" His features had coarsened with age, but he was still a good-looking man. And a bastard. How had she ever loved him? His fingers bit into her arm, hurting her.

"Get a life, Neil." Though she considered spitting in his face, she wasn't quite that brave or foolhardy. Neil had a wicked temper. "And let go of me." She jerked her arm out of his grasp.

"Maybe I should tell the good doctor what he's getting into." He pushed her back against the wall and smirked at her. "Or maybe you'll make it worth my while not to tell him."

"Not in this century. Go ahead and tell him," she said, her head held high. "It's common knowledge."

"Maybe so, but I'll bet he doesn't know the whole story. Come on, baby," he said, leaning down to kiss her neck. "Don't play so hard to get."

To hell with Neil's temper, she thought. "Oh, Neil," she said, fluttering her eyelashes at him. "I—I—" She ran her hand slowly down his chest until it rested on his belt buckle. "I think—" She hesitated and gazed at him, mutely appealing.

"Yeah?" He pressed closer. "What do you think, baby?"

"That you'd better chill out," she whispered, and dumped the contents of her glass down his pants.

Neil's face turned a livid red. Before she could move, he grabbed hold of her shoulders, his grip painful. "Bitch," he hissed. "You'll pay for that."

It was worth it, Piper thought, to give Neil back some of his own.

Eric hesitated at the door to the music room. Why should the news that Piper was in there with Croaker cause him a moment's doubt? A moment's mistrust, if he were honest. He was over Dawn, over her betrayal. There was no reason to let it interfere with his present relationship. No, he didn't distrust Piper, but her ex-fiancé was another matter.

He opened the door and saw Piper backed against the wall, Croaker's hands on her shoulders and her face lifted to his. The blow rolled through him like a kick in the stomach, hard, fast, and painful. Then he realized that Croaker's grip on her was anything but loverlike.

His guilt over mistrusting her deepened as he took in the front of Croaker's pants and her empty glass. "Need some help, Piper?"

They both looked at him, startled. Piper slipped away from Croaker and crossed to Eric's side. "Neil's under the delusion that he's human and not reptilian, Eric. Maybe you can recommend a psychiatrist who can disabuse him of that notion."

Red-faced, Croaker reached for her. "You little—"

"Give me an excuse, Croaker," Eric interrupted, slipping in front of Piper. "Just a whisper of an excuse, that's all I need."

"Don't, Eric. Let's go." Piper grabbed his arm, her fingers tightening on it. "He's not worth the trouble."

It wouldn't be any trouble to punch the bastard's lights out, Eric thought, but she didn't want him to.

"Don't ever touch her again, Croaker," he told the other man, and left before he lost it.

He dragged Piper into the first room he found. "Are you all right?" One hand on her shoulder, with the other he turned her face up to scrutinize it.

"I'm fine. That was amazingly satisfying. But"—she looked around the bathroom—"this isn't exactly the place to have a long discussion about it."

"Are you sure you don't want me to go back and punch him for you? Believe me, it would be my pleasure."

"You don't strike me as a violent man."

His fingers tightened briefly, then loosened as he slid his hands down her arms. "Normally I'm not." Did guilt have anything to do with his anger? He hoped not, but he wasn't sure. "What is it with that joker? That's the second time I've walked in and he's been hassling you. Those weren't the first incidents like that, were they?"

"You're very sweet," she said, touching his cheek.

"How many times, Piper? You can't even remember, can you? By God, I will go back and pound his face. That's the last time he's going to do it." He released her and reached for the door.

"Wait!" She grabbed his hand and tugged on it. "Defending me isn't necessary, but I appreciate it."

"It damn sure is."

"Do you think he's the first man I've ever had to discourage?"

"You slapped the hell out of him last time and that didn't discourage him."

She lifted a shoulder. "He's drunk. You'll only cause

a scene and then we'll never get out of here. Don't you want to leave? Would you rather fight or"—she smiled suggestively—"do something more pleasant?"

Eric frowned at her. "You play dirty, Angel. All right, you win. But if he does it again—"

She squeezed his arm. "Forget Neil. Let's go home."

They made their way back to the living room, where Piper found Marianne and gave her an excuse for their early departure. Judging from the knowing wink Marianne flung at Piper, Eric didn't think she'd fooled her friend for a minute.

He took Piper's hand as they walked to the car, still a little irritated that she had stopped him before he'd made sure Croaker didn't bother her again. He doubted his threat would linger long in the man's memory, especially since he was drunk. Cicadas chirred in the still twilight. Muted sounds of music, laughter, and talk drifted to him from the pool area out back, but the front entrance was deserted for the moment.

His fingers were on the car door when he heard Croaker's voice from behind them.

"Has she told you about her son's daddy? Has she told you she's a home wrecker who went after a married man?"

With an explosive oath, Eric whirled and started toward Croaker.

"Eric!" Piper grabbed his arm and hung on. "Don't!"

"Let me go, Piper. That's the last lie that bastard will spread about you, because I'm going to ram it down his throat."

"You can't," she said, her voice tight, almost tortured in its intensity.

"Why the hell can't I?"

She let go of his arm. Her chin lifted and she looked him squarely in the eye. "Because it's the truth."

EIGHT

"No," Eric said, staring at her. "I don't believe it." Piper and a married man? *His* Piper?

"It's true. Cole's father was married."

Vaguely aware that Croaker was still talking, Eric thought about punching him to shut him up. It didn't matter, though, the bomb had dropped. Abruptly, the background noise ceased.

Piper's face was pale, her lips trembled. She was upset, but dammit, so was he. "Did you plan to tell me? Ever?"

She averted her head. "Can we leave? I'd rather not discuss this here."

"No, I don't imagine you would," he said harshly. "And judging by the fact that you wouldn't be telling me now if your hand hadn't been forced—" He broke off and jerked open the car door. "Get in."

Neither of them spoke during the drive to his apartment. Though he told himself he should wait to hear her out, he couldn't stop the pain he felt. A married man. She had an affair with a married man. Bore a child as a result of that liaison. Piper had done that, she'd admitted it.

He'd thought they had the same values, believed in the same things. To find out that she had more in common with Dawn than with him . . . How could he have been so wrong about her? How could he have allowed himself to be taken in—again?

When they arrived at his place, he jammed the gearshift into park, wrenched the key from the ignition, and got out, not bothering to see if she followed. The way he felt right now, it might be better if she didn't.

"Could I have a drink?" She closed the apartment door behind her.

Silently, he poured her a bourbon, and one for himself. He took a long drink, peeled off his jacket, threw it on a chair. Jerked his tie loose while he watched her toss back a hefty swallow and choke on it. God, that beautiful, *innocent* face. Was it all a facade?

"Cole's father was married," she announced flatly. "With three children."

"That's all you're going to say?"

She spat the words out. "I had an affair with a married man. What more do you want to know?"

A muscle in his jaw twitched. "Did you know he was married?"

"I—" She twisted away from him, picking up her glass and downing most of what was left. Angrily, she turned back. "Will that make a difference? If I tell you, no, I didn't know he was married, does that make it okay? What if I say yes, Eric? Does that put me beyond the pale?"

"Dammit, Piper, don't take it out on me. I've got

more reason than you do to be angry about this." He wanted to heave his glass against the wall, but forced himself not to. Instead, he set it down, his jaw clenched against the need to shout. "You didn't tell me. Not even when—when I told you about Dawn, why didn't you tell me?"

"Are you so perfect? Haven't you ever made a mistake?"

Mistake? He'd married Dawn, hadn't he? Dawn, who had lied—and betrayed him. "Of course I have, but that isn't the point. The point isn't your affair with a married man either."

"The hell it's not. You're sitting in judgment of me because I had an affair with a married man."

"No, the point is you kept something from me that you knew would affect our relationship. That you knew was important to me, especially after what I told you yesterday."

"Yes, I did," she shot back. "Because I was afraid you'd react just as you're reacting. Sanctimonious, judgmental, self-righteous. Like you never made a mistake in your life. Did you ever cheat on Dawn?"

He shook his head. "No. I told you, I have a problem with adultery." He'd thought about it, even been tempted, but he hadn't done it. Because he had believed in the commitment, even if Dawn hadn't.

Piper picked up the phone and started to dial.

"What are you doing?" He snatched the receiver out of her hand.

Her chin lifted. "Calling my grandfather."

"I'll take you home. When we've finished."

"Don't bother. Judgmental bullies aren't my style."

Judgmental bully, was he? He slammed the phone down. "Because I asked you if you knew the man was married? I'm not trying to judge you, I'm trying to understand. My God, Piper, don't you realize that—I can't believe you would have done it if you'd known."

She laughed bitterly. "You're not judging me? Funny, it sure sounds like it to me. Let me set your mind at rest on one thing, then. As it happens, you're right. I didn't know he was married. In fact, he asked me to marry him before I even went to bed with him."

Relief swamped him. Thank God, she hadn't known. "I knew it had to be something like that."

She grabbed for the phone, but he held her off.

"So that makes you feel better?" she demanded, face flushed, chest heaving. "Can you justify sleeping with me? Now that you know I was merely stupid instead of immoral?"

"Dammit!" he shouted, losing the fight with his temper. He slammed the receiver down again and pounded his fist on the table. "You're putting words in my mouth."

"Are you going to tell me it doesn't bother you? That my affair with a married man doesn't bother you in the least?"

"Yes, it bothers me. Hell, yes, of course it bothers me. You knew it would, after Dawn."

Turning her back to him, she stood with her head bowed and her arms crossed over her chest. "Yes, I knew it would. But I hoped—Oh, it doesn't matter. Take me home."

Take her home. Let her leave, let her walk out of his life. Was that what he wanted? Piper hadn't known the man was married. Dawn had wrecked his life once already. Was he willing to let what happened with her color what happened now, with Piper? He remembered his surprise at Piper's inexperience. Whatever she had done, she was no practiced home wrecker. Young, naive—she'd made a mistake. Like Dawn had. But he hadn't been able to forgive Dawn.

"No, I don't want you to go," he said. He moved behind her, placing his hands on her shoulders. "We can work this out, Piper."

"Can we?" Her voice sounded wistful.

"Yes," he said softly, his mouth against her neck. He didn't want to end their relationship, he didn't want to lose her. He could accept it. Dawn's betrayal was in the past, he was over it. It had nothing to do with Piper. "Forgive me."

"I should have told you."

His hands covered her breasts. "It doesn't matter, it's in the past. We don't have to let it hurt us." Deftly, he unbuttoned her bodice and slid his hands inside her bra, fitting his palms against her bare breasts. Warm, heavy breasts.

"Eric, this isn't—"

He pressed up against her back, pulling her closer to him. Though he wasn't sure why, he knew it was important that he make love to her. Important that she understand he wanted her, and she wanted him.

"This isn't the answer. We should talk," she said faintly.

"Turn your head, let me kiss you," he murmured, his lips resting on her neck. He could feel her heartbeat, see her pulse fluttering frantically, the quick rise and fall of her chest. Her head turned and he kissed her, plunging his tongue inside her sweet, willing mouth.

When she tried to speak, he hushed her. "I want you, Piper. Let me make love to you."

"This won't solve . . . Oh, I . . . shouldn't," she whispered, sagging weakly against him, her head falling back against his shoulder.

But she would, he knew, and he slid her dress up.

Piper lay on Eric's chest, listening to his steady heartbeat, and damned herself as a fool. A fool to imagine that she could give herself to him, be with him, love him, and not fall in love with him. Why had it taken nearly losing him to realize it?

What did *he* feel? Did he care about her so much, he was willing to accept her past? A past that brought him far too close to the unhealed wound his wife's adultery had inflicted on him. Could he accept her past because she did matter to him . . . or because she didn't?

"Are you upset about what happened?" he murmured.

She rose on her elbow to look at him. "Because we had sex when we should have been talking?"

"Yeah." His fingers trailed over her cheek. "I'm not sure what happened there."

Neither was she. "Do you trust me?"

"You didn't know, Angel. The past is over, for both of us. Now is what matters."

He kissed her, began to make love to her again. Much later, she realized he'd never said that he trusted her.

❖━━━━━❖

Eric dragged himself to the office after releasing Virginia Johnson from the hospital. Normally, he didn't dread work as he had in Dallas before he left, but today . . . Today he knew he'd spend the day thinking about how he could have saved the Johnsons' baby.

Rubbing his temples, he remembered the long night, heard again Virginia's cries of pain as labor progressed, saw Randy's and Virginia's faces when they realized she would lose the baby. At twenty weeks, the baby hadn't stood a chance. None of the medicines, and he'd given Virginia everything he could, had halted her labor.

It was a mistake to become too emotionally involved with patients. Eric knew it and had done it anyway. Usually he managed to keep a good perspective, but practicing medicine in a small community was a lot different from the impersonal aspects of academic medicine. One of the reasons he'd left the university system and moved to Capistrano was because he wanted to treat people instead of cases. And though the rewards of his new practice were many, the flip side was bad too. When the flip side involved people he considered friends, it only made it that much harder.

There were no answers, but that didn't stop him from brooding about it. By noon he decided to cancel his lunch with Piper, certain he'd be lousy company. Cole's bouncing entry took that choice away.

"Hey, Doc!"

Impossible to respond to the kid without a smile, he thought. "Hey, Cole." They slapped palms. Eric watched the boy inspect the office, darting from one corner, to the plant stand, to another corner. "Why aren't you in school today?"

"Teachers hadda do something. Mom said she'd bring me to the L & M for a hamburger." He smacked his lips in anticipation.

"Where's your mother?"

"Talking to Effie. Can I ask you something? A flavor."

"A flavor?"

Cole nodded. "Will you be my dad?"

"Be your dad?" Eric stared at him with his mouth open. Good God, what was he supposed to say? He wasn't ready for marriage, he wasn't—

"At school," Cole continued. "Just for a day. Grandpa can't do it, so I'm asking you. Unless you don't want to." His lower lip trembled on his last sentence.

Mercifully, Eric's heart started beating again. A *favor*. For a school function, that's what Cole was talking about. "What is it you want me to do, Cole?"

"Next week they're having 'What my daddy does' day. We gotta get our dads to tell the class about their jobs. Grandpa says he can't do it this time. So, um, I know you're not my dad, but—well, could you?"

The kid had the biggest, brownest eyes Eric had ever seen. Absurdly touched, he wasn't sure how to answer him. "Does your mom know you're asking me?"

"No." Cole shook his head vigorously. "It makes her sad when they do daddy things at school and stuff. My daddy was a policeman, an *important* policeman. Bad guys shot him, but don't talk to Mommy about it, 'cause she'll cry."

"I'll be glad to talk to your class, but I need to make

sure it's all right with your mother first. She might not like it if I don't."

"You'll spoil it! Please? Do you hafta ask her?"

Something was wrong here, Eric mused. Cole was too anxious, even given the explanation. "Why don't you want me to tell her? Because she'll cry or because of something else?"

Cole hunched a shoulder. "I don't have a daddy. I made him up 'cause the other kids—" He broke off, suppressing a sob. "Sometimes I play like he was a fireman."

Careful, Eric, he told himself. Don't make it worse. "Everybody has a daddy, Cole. Even if you don't know much about him, you have a dad." What was Piper thinking, not to tell the child anything? "Have you asked your mom about him?"

"Sorta. She gets this sad look and then I feel bad, so mostly I don't."

Mostly he didn't. Poor kid. "I'll talk to your mom. Don't worry, I won't make her cry, I'll just ask her about visiting your class. Okay?"

"Great!" Magically, the tears disappeared.

"Eric?" Piper walked in. "Lord, Effie can talk. I see Cole's been entertaining you."

This discussion wouldn't wait, Eric decided. "Why don't you go ask Miss Effie to show you her magic tricks, Cole?"

" 'Kay." The boy ran out of the room.

Piper leaned against his desk. "I've been to see Virginia. Randy called me this morning and told me what happened."

Damn, he'd almost managed to forget that problem in the wake of his conversation with Cole. "How is she?"

"Depressed. I felt so useless, trying to comfort her. Nothing I said made any difference, nothing could make things better."

Eric nodded. "Depression is a normal reaction. Last night she was in too much shock for me to tell. And this morning when I released her, she was trying to be strong, I think for Randy's sake as much as her own. I wish—" He stopped and shook his head. No point going over it.

"Randy said you did everything you could."

"Yeah. But it wasn't enough." His head hurt, and he ran his hand across his brow. "They're taking it hard. You know how much the baby meant to them."

"They'll be all right. It'll just take them some time to adjust. Time to heal."

"Are you trying to comfort *me*, Piper?" he asked, smiling.

"Is there a law against that? You look upset." She walked over to him and laid a hand on his shoulder.

"Not nearly as much as Randy and Virginia," he said, covering her hand with his.

"But I can't do much for them. Maybe I can make you feel a little better."

"Look, it'll pass. I don't like it, but I'm used to it."

"Uh-huh." She pointed to the medical journal on his desk, opened to an article entitled "Premature Labor." "Don't try to brush it aside. You might be used to it, but it still bothers you."

With a shrug, he closed the journal. For some reason her concern, her care, made him uncomfortable. "Nobody likes to lose a patient." Pointedly, he changed the subject. "Cole asked me something a few minutes ago that we need to talk about."

"What's he up to now?"

Looking for a father, Eric thought. "He wanted me to talk to his class about my job. For a career day they're having."

"Do you mind? Is it a problem?"

"Piper, it's career day for fathers. He said Charlie couldn't do it, so he asked me."

Her face flamed. "Oh, God, I'm sorry. Cole didn't mean to put you on the spot like that. I'll just explain it to—"

"That's not it. I don't mind. I'm sure some of the other kids will ask family friends."

"And I'm sure several of them will have asked their mother's lover," she said dryly.

"If you don't want me to go, just say so. But you need to talk to Cole. Are you aware that he makes up stories about his father? That the other kids tease him about it? He thinks he doesn't have one because you've never told him about him."

"He *doesn't* have one," she stated flatly. "I've never told Cole about him because he'll never meet him or know him."

"But surely—"

"Eric," she interrupted. "I appreciate your interest in Cole, but this is really none of your business. He is *my* son and I'll do what I think is best for him."

"It became my business when he talked to me. I can't ignore what he told me. He needs to know, Piper. Something, at least."

"How dare you presume to know what's best for Cole? You've only known him a few weeks. I'm his mother."

"Which is precisely why you're being so irrational. However much the man hurt you, he's still Cole's father. Have you thought about what will happen as the boy gets older? He won't always leave it alone because it makes you cry. What if someone else tells him something?"

She stared at him, a stricken expression in her eyes. "You don't understand. You're trying to help, I know, but you don't understand. Please, Eric, just leave it alone. Believe me when I tell you that Cole's not ready to hear the story."

"What about me? When are you going to tell me what happened?"

"You're not ready to hear it, either."

NINE

Virginia Johnson stood hesitantly at the door to Piper's greenhouse. "I'm so glad to see you, Virginia," Piper said. "How are you?" It had only been a week since the miscarriage and Piper thought Virginia looked worse than she had immediately afterward.

"Getting by, I guess. Are you busy?"

"Of course not. Sit down and talk to me while I finish with this violet. I've been putting off pruning for far too long."

Virginia sat in the chair next to her and said nothing, pleating her skirt nervously.

"How is Randy?" Piper ventured after a moment.

"Randy is a mess, and so am I."

Piper took her hands in a sympathetic gesture. "I wish there was something I could do."

"There is. Give us that remedy again." Her eyes implored. "I know that Dr. Chambers doesn't think it worked, but it did. And I want Randy to have it so that when I'm recovered we can try again. Otherwise—well, it will be pointless without the remedy."

With a sigh, Piper let go of her hands. "Have you talked to Eric about it?"

"He's been changing Randy's medicine ever since we used up all of your remedy, but nothing works. I'm desperate." She clutched her shirt at her breast, her eyes wide and glistening with emotion.

Oh, Lord, what was she supposed to do? "I can't give it to you without Eric's knowledge."

"Can't or won't?"

Piper paced the room to avoid looking at Virginia's beseeching expression. "You know Eric and I are involved. He'll never speak to me again if I go behind his back to do this."

"Then don't go behind his back. Convince him that at the least, it's harmless. Please."

Piper passed her hand over her eyes. This was going to blow up in her face, but there was no way she could resist her friend's desperate pleading. "All right, I'll talk to him, but I can't promise it will do any good."

Virginia rose. "I don't want to make problems between you two, but we're—"

"Desperate. I know. I'll talk to Eric tonight."

"Thank you, Piper." Virginia grasped her hands. "You can't imagine what this means to us."

"Oh, yes I can," Piper murmured as the door closed behind Virginia. "That's why I'm going to talk to him."

As luck would have it, Eric was coming over that night for dinner. After she'd cleaned the kitchen Piper walked into the living room to find Eric and Cole wrestling. "Who's winning?"

"So far," Eric panted, grabbing both of Cole's wrists in one hand, "it's a draw."

Pure longing pierced her as she watched them roughhouse. They looked so natural together, like father and son. Once again she wondered why Eric didn't have children of his own. He'd make a wonderful father. With difficulty, she shook off the mood. "It's past bedtime, son."

"Mo-om," he said, drawing the word out, "I was gonna win."

"Come on, sport." Eric stood and turned Cole upside down to carry him to his room. "Better luck next time."

"Next time," she heard her son say, "you have to keep one hand behind your back."

"It's a deal. Hey, no grabbing my leg while I'm walking. If I go down, so do you."

Cole giggled.

The longing came back, with a vengeance.

"That kid's going to go far," Eric said when he returned a few minutes later. "I've agreed to a match I can't possibly win."

"You'll handle it, I bet," she said, leading the way to the front porch and sitting on the swing. "You seem to know just how to deal with him. Why didn't you ever—" She stopped in midsentence, aghast at what she'd been about to ask him. Thinking it was one thing, asking him was another. Forbidden territory. Oh, not that he'd said it, but it was implied.

He sat beside her and touched her cheek. "You can finish the question," he told her. When she said nothing, he finished it for her. "You wanted to know why I don't have any kids."

"Yes. But you don't have to talk about it."

He shrugged. "Dawn isn't exactly the maternal type, for one thing. At first, I wasn't in a big hurry to have kids and later—" He shrugged again. "Later I was glad we didn't have any."

"I didn't mean to pry," she said, uncomfortable with the subject.

"You're not prying. But I can think of things I'd rather do than talk about Dawn."

"What things?" she asked, and kissed him lightly. It began lightly anyway, but it seemed Eric had other ideas. With something between a laugh and a groan, Piper pulled her mouth away from his. "I can't think when you kiss me like that."

"So who needs to think?" His arms tightened around her as he looked at her. "Maybe we should go to my place."

"Good idea, but I can't. I've got to get up early tomorrow."

"Are you sure?" He started kissing the side of her neck.

"Maybe for a little while . . ." Except that she knew it wouldn't be a little while if she went with him. It never was. Then she remembered Virginia and tensed in his arms.

He drew back to look at her. "What's wrong? All of a sudden you're stretched tight as a bowstring."

"We need to talk."

He studied her. "I'm not going to like this, am I?" She shook her head. "Is it that bad?" He settled back with his arm around her shoulders.

"Virginia came to see me today."

"Any special reason?" His fingers trailed up her neck.

"They want my herbal remedy again." She felt his fingers tighten on her nape. "But I told her I couldn't give it to them without talking to you first."

"Piper—"

"You don't believe it worked," she said in a rush, "but the point is, they do. Maybe it will help them. Let me try."

"That's not the point. I don't have a problem with them trying it again."

She stared at him, her mouth agape. "You don't?"

"Not necessarily. As long as I'm sure it won't harm him. I have to know what's in it before we can go any further."

"I told you—"

He held up a hand. "You said it wasn't made to be ingested. Do you seriously expect me to prescribe a drug for one of my patients when I know nothing about it?"

"It's not a drug for you to prescribe, it's an herbal remedy. There's nothing wrong with my giving them an herbal remedy."

"No way, Angel," he said, shaking his head. "Randy's on other medications. Your remedy could interact poorly with what he's already taking. Tell me what's in it and let me look into it."

"There shouldn't be anything in it that would hurt him. Oh, maybe the orchid, but—"

"Orchid?" he interrupted. "Some orchids are toxic, at least to a degree."

"A very minute quantity," she assured him. "Apparently, it didn't bother him before."

"You're stalling. Are you going to tell me what's in it or not?"

Piper stood, walking over to lean against the porch railing and stare out at the moonlit pasture, at the low, rolling hills in the distance that gave way to the taller mountains. She saw the dark shapes of the cattle, settling in along the foothills for the night, a soothing scene that usually made her feel better, but didn't now. "If I want to help them I don't have a choice, do I?" she said finally.

Eric came to stand behind her. "Can't you trust me on this? What do you think I'm going to do with it?"

"You want to send it to Dave."

"Only with your permission." When she said nothing, he asked indignantly, "Do you really think I'd betray your confidence like that?"

"No, of course not, but you still think I should let him have it."

He put his hands on her shoulders and turned her to face him. "I've thought that from the first. You owe it to yourself and to others like the Johnsons to let Dave research it."

"I'm afraid."

His gaze was sincere, intent. "Why? What is it that frightens you about it?"

"The publicity. If this gets out—"

"Why should it? Dave can keep a confidence."

"What if it works, Eric? What if it's a success? Dave will have to make it public if he's going to help anyone. And I guarantee you that they'll trace the origin of the remedy right straight back to me." She pulled away and began to pace the porch.

He studied her while she paced. "Don't you think it's time you told me about this phobia you have of publicity?"

"Phobia? It's a very reasonable fear."

"Reasonable? Why?"

"Because of my past," she burst out. "Because I've been hounded by the media before, and I won't go through it again. Or put Cole through it."

"What happened?" he asked softly.

"You know what happened."

"Not the details."

Her hands tightened into fists. "Eric, I can't—I can't talk about it."

"It's not going to make a difference in our relationship, if that's what's bothering you. Your past doesn't matter to me, you should know that by now. Don't you know how much I—" He stopped. "I care about you, Piper."

Cared about her, she thought. Not loved her, cared about her. And God knows, he didn't trust her. Discovering that he didn't love her hurt, more than it should have. Great sex, no strings attached. Wasn't that what she'd wanted at first? Wasn't that all she'd been ready to give? Could he help it that she'd changed the plan and fallen in love with him?

She forced herself to unclench her fists. "I'll go write it down for you. You can send it to Dave tomorrow."

"You don't have to do this."

"Yes, I do." She sighed and shoved a hand through her hair, which fell back in its usual wild disarray. "I just hope it doesn't turn out like I think it will."

"Nothing bad is going to happen. Why can't you believe that?"

She gripped the porch rail and gazed at the fields again. "Because in my experience, something bad always does happen."

Piper was the only woman Eric had ever known who could drive him to insomnia. Once they'd become lovers, he'd thought insomnia was a thing of the past. But there he was, lying in bed alone and trying not to think about what had happened that evening. He'd been within an inch of telling her he loved her. He wasn't sure how he felt about that.

What had happened with that married man that was so terrible she couldn't tell him? He'd thought once he knew the basic facts, she would tell him the rest of it. Had it really been spread all over the papers? Or was Piper overreacting?

He would warn Dave of the need for discretion, but he didn't feel it was really necessary. As physicians, both of them were accustomed to dealing with confidential matters. Piper had nothing to fear.

The next morning, after he'd talked to Dave, Eric called her. "The recipe is fine, except the orchid can cause nausea, vomiting, and a few other uncomfortable symptoms. Is it really necessary?"

"For all I know the orchid is the thing that makes it work."

"Hmm. Still, I'd rather you dropped it."

"Fine. Are you saying I can give it to Virginia?"

"Yes, I'll call her myself. I want to make sure Randy lets me keep an eye on him."

"Did you send it to Dave?"

He could hear the tension in her voice. "Talked to him this morning. Don't worry, Angel, he understands the need for confidentiality. Dave won't let a soul know."

"He'd better not."

Her doubt was tangible, he could feel it, emanating from the phone line. "Trust me on this, I won't let it hurt you."

"Famous last words."

"Piper—"

"It's done, Eric. Listen, I've got to go to a flower show in San Antonio this weekend. Do you want to come with me?"

An effective way to kill the subject, he thought. "You and me in San Antonio? Alone?"

She laughed. "Except for several thousand plant enthusiasts. It's a working weekend for me. But I'm free at night."

Two nights with Piper with no beepers, children, or grandfathers? "Forrest owes me. I'll get him to cover for me."

"Good. I was hoping you could come."

"Angel, there wasn't a chance I'd have turned you down." He hung up, deciding his uneasiness over the remedy was simply a reflection of Piper's. He trusted Dave. Nothing bad would happen.

❦━━━━━❦

"Are you trying to break your back, Piper?" Eric grabbed one side of the heavy box she was dragging to her booth and pulled with her.

"If we ever want to eat tonight, we've got to get this set up." She accepted his help but continued tugging on the box.

"God knows that kid you hired is young enough and strong enough to handle it. Where is he?"

"Doing something else. Besides, this isn't really"—she panted as they heaved the box onto the table—"heavy."

"Yeah? Then why do I have a hernia?" He hadn't realized just how much physical labor Piper's work involved. And until a few days ago, he hadn't realized just how much time she spent trying to expand her business without overextending herself. He studied her for a minute. "Is this show so important? You're as nervous as I've ever seen you."

She wiped sweat from her brow. "If I can hook that chain I told you about, my business will take off like honeysuckle growing on a fence. The owner's a tough sell."

Eric looked at her display. "You've got great flowers. What's the problem?"

"Lots of folks have good flowers. Mine have to be the best."

Eric understood that drive to succeed. He liked the fact that Piper didn't wait around for opportunities to come to her, but went after them herself. "But yours are unique." He gestured toward them. "Look around, it's obvious."

"What's obvious is that there's lots of competition."

He slipped an arm around her waist and squeezed lightly. "I can see you need me to prescribe something to settle your nerves. I know just the thing."

She glanced at him sideways. "Oh, and what would that be?"

"We start," he murmured in her ear, "by having a romantic dinner. Then I take you for a stroll along the Riverwalk."

Stretching her neck, she gave a tiny groan. "That sounds good. What happens then?"

"I don't think I'd better tell you here," he said, wishing the booth weren't so public. "It'll have to be discussed in a private consultation."

She smiled, her eyes holding a promise of the night to come. "Sounds like my kind of medicine, Doc."

By habit, Eric woke early the next morning. Piper slept with her hips cradled against him, his hand resting over one satin-smooth breast. Nice, he thought. Not having to take her home in the middle of the night, making love as much as they wanted, having her there when he woke in the morning. That last thought jolted him wide awake.

He was in love with her, dammit. Love, not just lust. Absolutely, positively, totally in love with her. Why hadn't he broken things off when he suspected he was falling for her? He'd thought he could handle it, thought he could keep himself from getting in too deep. Or told himself he could because he couldn't face losing her.

He'd never been so glad to hear an alarm go off.

"Tell me I'm dreaming that sound," Piper mumbled.

"Afraid not, Angel. Time to get up."

"Don't tell me you're one of those disgustingly cheerful morning people," she said, sitting up.

"Guilty." Realizing he was in love with Piper hadn't decreased his desire for her. Lightly, he ran his hand up her spine and bit back a sigh of regret. He couldn't make her late this morning. The show was too important to her.

She aimed a provocative look at him over her shoulder. "Even when you haven't slept?"

"That depends on why." Her hair tumbled in disarray over her shoulders and down her bare back. "Besides, we slept," he said, drawing her to him and kissing her. "Some." He started caressing her breast.

"I've got to get dressed," she said, inhaling sharply. She leaned over to kiss him again. "Right now." Her hands strayed over his chest.

"Then you'd better go while you can."

Sparing him a regretful glance, she left the bed. His gaze took in the tousled hair, rosy cheeks, lush glowing curves. He shut his eyes. "Go away, Angel, before I make you very late."

TEN

Eric spent the morning at the show with Piper and the rest of the afternoon with Dave. He knew she wouldn't miss him. She'd be too busy trying to get that big contract, as well as checking out her competition. Since this particular show only ran for a day, she'd cram something into every minute.

When he arrived at Piper's booth late that afternoon he found her reaching over a wide table for an orchid. For every inch she stretched, her skirt rose a little higher. The joker standing beside her was giving her his full attention.

"Hi," Eric said, grabbing the plant before it fell from the table. "Did you think I'd bailed out?"

"Of course not." She straightened and took the orchid from him, and her skirt slid back down several inches, he noted with relief and a small jab of irritation. She set the plant down close to her and drew his arm through hers. Pleased, he noticed the gesture wasn't lost on the other man. "Eric, this is Mr. McKinnley, the owner of Bloomers, the chain I was telling you about."

"Greg, please," the man said, extending a hand to him.

"Eric Chambers." McKinnley didn't look anything like Eric's conception of the owner of a chain of nurseries. A huge, powerfully built blond, he would have looked equally at home on a football field or in a gymnasium lifting weights. Here, among thousands of plants and flowers, he merely looked incongruous.

"Greg is interested in marketing my hybrids, Eric. And some of my other plants too."

"I'd really like to discuss the deal in further detail," McKinnley said. "What do you say we do it over dinner?"

Piper shot an agonized glance at Eric. Bye-bye romantic dinner, he thought, but if McKinnley thought he would bow out and leave the blond man with Piper, he was certifiable. "Would you like to join us at the Bayous?" he asked, sliding an arm around Piper's waist. The grateful smile she threw him went a long way toward making up for his concession.

"Yes, please do, Greg," she said.

Eric gave McKinnley points for taking it like a gentleman. He grinned and said, "Maybe tomorrow morning would be better."

"We insist." Eric wished he didn't know how important this deal was to Piper. Mentally he consigned Greg McKinnley to the devil.

They met McKinnley at the restaurant, one reputed to have the best gumbo on the river. Eric wished Piper had chosen something less striking to wear. Her sleeveless green dress came up almost to her neck in the front, plunged low in the back, and showed off legs that belonged on a much taller person. McKinnley would have to be blind not to appreciate the effect.

Not blind, but smooth, Eric acknowledged. Within five minutes of their sitting down, he knew Eric's profession, how long he'd lived in Capistrano, and he'd gathered a fair idea of Piper and Eric's relationship. Then he turned his attention to Piper, and there it stayed for the rest of the evening.

After they'd finished eating, Piper excused herself, leaving the two men alone for the first time. "What brought you to Capistrano?" McKinnley asked him. "A small west Texas town doesn't seem like it would suit you."

Eric shrugged. "I'd been in the university system for a long time and was ready for a change."

"Have you known Piper long?" He asked it casually, and sipped his drink.

Eric met his eyes. "Long enough."

McKinnley tapped his fingers on his glass. "I don't suppose you and Piper are going your separate ways come Monday morning?"

He sure cut to the chase, Eric thought. "Guess again." He took a healthy swallow of his gin and tonic.

"Involved?" McKinnley hazarded.

"You got it."

"Exclusively involved?" he persisted, leaning forward.

"Bingo."

"Damn, I was afraid of that." He sat back in his chair

and downed half of his drink. "Piper's a beautiful woman."

"Yes." Eric waited to see what else McKinnley had to say. Somehow, he didn't think he was finished.

"You know, since we're doing business now, I'll be in touch with Piper frequently. I'm bound to hear if you two, say, have a misunderstanding."

"Don't hold your breath," Eric told him.

McKinnley laughed. "I wouldn't give her up either. You'd have to be crazy to do that, and you don't look crazy to me."

Just about Piper, Eric thought. And he was a lot further gone than he wanted to be.

"I can't believe it!" Piper exclaimed as she and Eric left the restaurant. She threw her arms around Eric's neck and hugged him, eager to share her happiness, but he didn't seem very happy. She figured he was upset because his plans for a romantic dinner with just the two of them had been spoiled. "I know you'd wanted to be alone and so did I, but this was very important to my business."

Irritation flickered over his face. "Why do you think I invited him along?"

"You're angry."

"What makes you think I'm angry?"

"Well, for starters you're walking a hundred miles an hour. Could you slow down?" She was practically sprinting to keep up with him.

"Sorry." He slowed, but not much. They were approaching their hotel when he said, "Why did you wear that dress?"

Puzzled, she looked down. "Don't you like it?"

"It's too short. And too low in the back."

"You didn't mind earlier," she snapped, remembering how they nearly hadn't made it out of the room in time for dinner.

"This was a business dinner."

"So?" She stared at him incredulously.

"He might have been able to keep his eyes off you if you—" Eric broke off, gritting his teeth. "Never mind."

"So that's what this is about," she said slowly. "Am I supposed to wear sackcloth and ashes so no man will look at me?"

"Give me a break." He glared at her, his gaze encompassing her from head to toe. "It seems like you could have worn something more businesslike to a business dinner."

"My dress is plenty businesslike," she shot back, her temper firing. "Greg didn't have a problem talking business."

"Greg was just a perfect gentleman, wasn't he?"

Furious by now, she forced herself not to shout. "I know when a man is talking business and when he's making a pass at me. And Greg didn't. So you can stop with this irrational jealousy." She strode into the lobby ahead of him.

He caught up to her as she stepped into the elevator. The door closed. "Irrational?" He backed her against the wall and grated out, "Let me tell you something, Angel. If I hadn't been glued against your side with my hand on your thigh, you would've seen more passes than Troy Aikman throws in a season."

The elevator door opened. Piper didn't speak as they walked to the room. Once inside, she threw down her purse and said, her voice dangerously calm, "Don't you *ever* insinuate that I use my looks to get ahead in business. How dare you say that to me?"

"All I'm saying is that while you may have had business on your mind, that's not all that McKinnley was thinking about."

"If that's true, it's not my fault."

"You can't help it that you're so damned beautiful, can you?"

She leveled a long stare at him. "Tell me something, Eric. What was the first thing you noticed about me?"

He gritted his teeth. "That's beside the point."

"No, it is the point. Do you think I like it that most men never see beyond my looks?"

"I don't know," he fired back. "Do you?" Staring at her, his eyes glittered, dark green and angry.

"You're making a federal case out of nothing. Greg was perfectly polite."

He gave a short bark of laughter. "Yeah, he perfectly politely asked my permission to put the moves on you."

Piper's mouth dropped open. "He—he asked you if he—"

Eric caged her in by slapping his palms against the wall on either side of her head. Glaring down at her, his voice low and dark, he said, "Yeah. As in, can I have a shot at her if you're not involved?"

She couldn't swallow, or breathe. "What did you tell him?"

"I told him it was up to you." Their bodies not quite touching, the heat of temper and passion rose between them.

"You did?" Blood heated in her veins, and her heart beat a fast cadence of desire that warred with the anger.

"Hell, no," he said. "I told him you were mine." His mouth descended on hers in a hard, savage kiss, possessing her with a hunger and barely leashed violence she'd never felt before.

She was achingly, vibrantly aware of him, of the fire of his mouth as he took hers, of every taut angle of his body, of each rippling, smooth muscle beneath his clothes. He lifted her up, so that his hardness pressed against the cleft of her thighs. She damned herself for not resisting him when she was angry, yet she locked her arms around his neck and pressed her breasts into his chest. Wrenching her mouth away, she searched his eyes and whispered, "Am I yours?"

"Yes," he muttered, and ravaged her mouth again. "Yes, dammit, yes." He slid her leg up around his hip and pulled her even more tightly against him. He found her breast beneath the soft fabric and drew in his breath when his palm settled on the bare skin. His other hand slid beneath the short skirt to caress her thighs, her hips, to feel the telltale moisture.

Waves of pleasure lapped her, making her quiver, making her burn. She couldn't think, could only feel, as his hands and lips and the hard feel of his body against hers drew a response she was powerless to halt. He let her slide down until her feet were on the floor again. Her legs felt weak, ready to buckle at any moment.

"I can't go through it again, Piper." His hands ran

over her urgently, possessively. He stared at her, then he crushed her mouth under his. Unhooking the top of her dress, he dragged it down and buried his face in her breasts. "I need you," he said, his voice hoarse and muffled against her skin.

"And I need you." She helped him draw her hose and panties off before he flung them against the wall. Her fingers grappled with his to strip his shirt and throw it aside, to rip her dress all the way down and off. Her breath came in quick bursts, she heard the thunder of her heartbeat as her hands reached out to him to unbutton, unzip, quickly, desperately.

Over and over, he plundered her mouth, kissing her neck, feasting on her breasts, then he bore her down on the bed. He molded her skin, his hands and mouth racing over her, burning, igniting explosions of sensation that fed on the touch of his hands, the touch of his mouth, the heat of his body. Then he slid his hands down her thighs in a sensual caress that made her body ripple, straining and eager to be one with him.

His eyes were dark as he looked down at her. She felt the passion as if it were a drug pumping through her blood. Her breath came so unevenly she thought she might faint from the rapid pulsing beat of it, and when she put her hands on his chest, she felt the same raging cadence in him. As he plunged inside her his mouth possessed hers, muffling her cry. Then he lifted his head and watched her as he thrust into her, taking her fast and fierce. She moved with him, her arms and legs tight around him, as wild and reckless as he, until she hung on the razor's edge of desire. With a last powerful lunge he sent her over and she shattered, his cry of release echoing in her mind as his shudders died away within her body.

Later, much later, her heart wept. Because she loved him and he would never trust her.

"Did I hurt you?" he asked. "I wasn't . . . gentle." He stroked her hair, softly, lightly.

"Neither was I." She rolled onto her back and turned her head to look at him. "It was—" She stopped, realizing she couldn't describe it without telling him she loved him.

He sighed. "Yeah," he said, and lowered his mouth to hers.

"What do you mean it works? Piper's herbal remedy is a cure for impotence? Why didn't you tell me this last week, when I was in San Antonio?" It was the last thing Eric had expected to hear when he answered the call from Dave. He couldn't believe he'd heard him correctly. Surely the phone lines had crossed.

"We just found out," Dave said. "It appears to boost testosterone production, increasing sperm count. We're also trying it as an additive in the new injection."

"The latest 'miracle cure,'" Eric said sarcastically. Randy Johnson was one of the unlucky fifteen percent the new injection didn't work for. Another failure. Eric didn't like failures. Neither did Dave.

"In eighty-five percent of the cases, it is a miracle cure. I'm as sorry as you are it didn't work for Randy."

"I know you had hopes for it too, Dave. But what does Piper's remedy have to do with the injection?"

"We want to see if we can help the other fifteen

percent. It will have to be tested extensively, of course, but there's a chance for success. You want to tell Piper yourself?"

Eric didn't think Piper would be pleased. "No, but I guess I'd better. You know how worried she is about publicity. This development just means more chance of word leaking out. Boosting testosterone production is something in itself. If it has an effect on that injection—"

"Tell her to relax. Nothing will be made public without her permission." Dave paused and added, "But there's a very real possibility that Piper will be involved with the 'miracle drug.' Hard to avoid publicity in that case."

Though he debated whether to tell her then or to wait until they knew more about the remedy's effects on the injection, ultimately, Eric decided she should be kept abreast of the news as it developed.

It was chilly that night, but they sat out on her porch swing because it was one of the few places they could talk privately. After Cole went to bed, anyway. Until then no place was private.

"It might work?" she repeated after he told her. She shoved her hands through her hair and dropped her head down. After a moment she looked at him. "Great. I can see the media in their feeding frenzy now. Is it too late for me to withdraw permission to use it?"

He nodded. "Much too late. Dave could be wrong, you know, it might be just a flash in the pan. Don't worry yet. They haven't even begun to experiment with the new injection."

"I can't help but worry about it. You don't understand."

"And I won't until you tell me the whole story." When she started to speak, he covered her lips with his fingers. "I'm not arguing about that again tonight, I know it's useless." Which reminded him of another sore subject. "Have you reconsidered telling Cole about his father?"

"No. He'll learn about him when I decide he's ready, and he's not ready."

"Angel, I know it's going to be hard to tell him, but you have to eventually."

"We've been through this before and I haven't changed my mind. Are you trying to start a fight with me?"

"No, I'm attempting to have an adult conversation with you." Which she was making extremely difficult.

"So now I'm childish because I don't agree with you?"

Eric threw his hands in the air. "I don't know why I bother to talk to you when I can see your mind is closed."

"Me neither."

He smiled, reluctantly. "Fighting wasn't what I had in mind when I came over."

"What did you have in mind, Doc?" she drawled, leaning back in the swing.

"Something a lot more fun." He slipped an arm around her and nuzzled her neck. They hadn't been alone together much since returning from San Antonio, which was primarily his fault. The trip—what had happened after their dinner with McKinnley—had exposed an issue he didn't want to deal with. His reaction to McKinnley's pursuit of Piper had made it crystal clear that he wasn't over Dawn's betrayal. Eric hated that Dawn had the power, even now, to jeopardize his future with Piper. Consequently, rather than think much about it, he'd buried himself in work since returning.

Piper tapped a finger on his chest. "I can read you like tea leaves. What would you say to a guided tour?"

"Depends on what we're touring."

"The greenhouse." Her fingers walked down his chest. "Among other things."

He sucked in his breath when she reached the waistband of his pants. "I think I might be up for that."

She smiled. "I'm counting on it."

ELEVEN

Piper stalked into Eric's office and slapped her palms down on his desk. Leaning over until she was in his face, she grated out, "You just had to talk me into it, didn't you? 'You owe it to yourself, Piper, and to the others you might help.'"

Eric stared at her, totally perplexed. "Clue me in here, Angel."

"I'm not your 'Angel.' If you say that to me one more time, I swear I'll lay you out. Don't think I can't do it, either. Sam taught me how to protect myself when I was eleven years old." She glared at him, looking very much like she might go ahead and make good on her threat. "I told you this would happen, but you wouldn't listen to me. God, I should have known better than to have trusted you. I *did* know better." She spun on her heel away from the desk and slapped the newspaper she carried against her palm.

Eric stood and took a step toward her. "What's the matter with you?" He reached out a hand to her, but she froze him with a look he'd never even imagined she could give him.

"Don't touch me." Her voice was low, quiet, and as cold as he'd ever heard it. "Don't you dare."

"What is it? What's wrong?"

"So Dave knows how to keep a secret," she said, all but sneering. "Isn't that what you told me? That he wouldn't betray my confidence and neither would you?"

"Yes, and neither of us would, Piper."

"Explain *that*." She threw the paper down on his desk.

Eric spread it out. Heading an article entitled "Beautiful Herbalist Discovers Aphrodisiac!" was Piper's picture—a younger Piper, but still recognizable. Beneath the headline the story began, " 'Lolita of the West' is mystery herbalist with a startling new discovery."

He raised his eyes to look at her. "I don't understand."

"Dave sprung a leak."

" 'Lolita of . . .' " His voice trailed off as he gazed down at the paper, then looked at her again. "God, no."

"Precisely. The Lubbock papers weren't the only ones to run stories about the hussy who ruined Dr. Roger Griffin's life." She tapped her chest. "You're looking at her."

He simply stared at her. Piper continued, her words cracking through the air like the lash of a whip. "Seven years. Seven years and now it comes back to haunt me."

"I don't believe it," he said flatly.

Effie knocked on the door and poked her head in. "Doctor, there's a man out here who says he's a reporter. He wants to talk to you."

"So, you didn't know a thing about it," Piper said.

Eric stared at Piper incredulously before he remembered Effie's presence. "Tell him to forget it. And Effie, cancel anything else I've got today."

"Yes, Doctor." Effie left in a hurry.

"Don't cancel on my account," Piper said sarcastically. "The public deserves to know, after all. Five more minutes and I'll have said everything I want to say to you."

"Wait just a damn minute." He grabbed her arm, holding her until she looked at him. "Do you think that I leaked this story to the press?"

"Somebody did."

Fury surged through him. She must have seen it in his eyes because she took a step back, but she still stood with her chin angled up, ready for a fight. "If that's the opinion you have of my ethics," he asked her, "then why in the hell have you been sleeping with me?"

"Why shouldn't I? Did you expect anything different from the 'Lolita of the West'?"

"I asked you a question. Is that what you really think, that I sold the story to the press?"

For a long moment her gaze locked with his, then she dropped her eyes. "No."

Though his grip relaxed, he still held her. "Piper, talk to me. Tell me what really happened."

Glancing back up at him, she opened her eyes wide. "Surely you read it. Wasn't it in the Dallas papers? Or were you in San Antonio then? Well, no matter, I'm sure they ran it there too. But let me refresh your memory. I'm the woman who destroyed the famous cardiologist,

Dr. Roger Griffin, and drove his wife to attempt murder."

"Tell me the truth, not what the papers wrote."

"Why should I tell you anything at all? What are you doing?" she asked him when he picked up the phone.

"Calling Dave," he said grimly. "Sit down and let me get to the bottom of this."

"It's simple. Either Dave or somebody at his clinic sold the story to the papers for a tidy sum and then the reporters did what they do best. They dug up all the dirt. Not that it would be hard to do. Reporters have long memories and I made the mistake of not changing my name."

Eric punched angrily at the phone buttons. "Dr. Chambers calling for Dr. Burson. He'll talk to me." Under his breath, he added, "He damned well better."

He gazed at Piper's back as she turned to stare out the window. Seven years ago. He remembered, of course. The story had run in every paper in the state, and quite a few outside of it. And the tabloids had loved it.

"Dave? I'm looking at the front page of the paper. What the hell happened?"

"I don't know," Dave said, "I just read it an hour ago. Obviously I've got a leak. When I find out who, heads are going to roll."

"Fat lot of good that does Piper. The reporters are already snapping at our heels here."

"Eric, is Piper really—"

"I haven't talked to her yet," he interrupted, risking a glance at her. She stood motionless at the window.

"As soon as I find out anything, I'll call you. Tell Piper I'm sorry."

"Right," he said. "That'll help." Eric hung up and turned to Piper, trying to marshal his thoughts. "Your media phobia—"

"Merited, wouldn't you say?" she interrupted.

"Apparently. What happened, Piper?" he asked again, his voice gentle. "Tell me." It hurt him to look at her, to see her pain.

She shrugged and faced him. "More or less what the papers said. Cole's father is Dr. Roger Griffin. Surely you've heard of him."

He nodded, his gaze locked with hers. "He developed one of the leading prosthetic valves for the heart."

"That's him, Roger Griffin, wonder of the medical world. His wife found out about our affair and came after us with a gun. She missed me and hit him. The state tried her for attempted murder."

"And you took the fall."

"The defense put me on the stand and tore me into little shreds. They painted *her* as a desperate woman trying to save her family." She flourished her hand. "They had three kids, by the way."

"So you said. And they portrayed you as a gold digger eager to hook a rich and famous doctor. A Lolita out for anything she could get."

"There you have it. I see you're remembering it now. Of course, I was a little old to be a Lolita, but the press didn't care much about accuracy."

"Now tell me the truth."

"How do you know that isn't the truth?" Her head held high, she faced him across the room.

Eric shook his head. "Because I know you. Don't, Piper. Just talk to me." He could see the despair in her eyes, the pain that showed through the anger. "You didn't know he was married, so I assume you didn't know who he was, either."

"It doesn't matter now."

"If only I'd listened to you—"

"You were so convinced you were right, that nothing would go wrong. And I knew something bad would happen. I knew it and still, I let you talk me into giving Dave that remedy. God, why did I listen to you?"

"I'd give anything if this hadn't happened. I'll talk to the press, tell them the story is a lie. We'll work it out, Piper."

"No, Eric. Not this time." She walked toward the door.

He stepped in front of it, blocking her way. "What are you saying?"

"It's over. We won't work anything out."

"Don't do this. This is a mistake."

"Oh, no, I already made the mistake. The day I got involved with you." Sadly, she looked at him. "You see, I knew better, but I did it anyway. And now I'm paying."

He moved from in front of the door, but grabbed her arm as she started by. "Don't, Piper. Please don't go. Let me help."

"You can't. No one can. Now let me go, Eric."

He dropped her arm. Piper walked out.

The phone was ringing when she got home. Piper let the answering machine pick up the call, but she listened in on the slim chance it was someone she actually wanted to talk to. When she recognized Janie Settle, the principal of Cole's school and an old friend of hers, she answered.

"Janie," she said as she grabbed the phone, "is something wrong with Cole?"

"You'd better get down here, Piper. He's been fighting."

"Oh, Lord, I'll be right there."

Ten minutes later she walked into the principal's office. "What happened? Why was he fighting?" she asked Janie, sinking into a chair.

"I haven't been able to find that out. Cole isn't being cooperative, to say the least." Janie went to the door and called Cole in.

Piper looked at him and her heart twisted. His lip was split, his eye bruised. Dried blood stained his face and the front of his shirt. His posture stated anger, rather than contrition.

"What happened, Cole?"

Silently defiant, he hunched a shoulder.

"Tell me, son." He scuffed his shoe on the floor. "Mrs. Settle, if I could talk to him alone, I might get it out of him."

"If you can't get a satisfactory answer from him," Janie said, "we'll have to suspend him for the rest of the day."

"He'll talk to me." She hoped. The principal left. "Tell me now," Piper said.

Frowning mutinously, Cole looked at his mother. "They called you names. And me. So I hit 'em."

"What kind of names?" she asked, although she had a sinking feeling she knew.

"Billy Paxton said I was a bastard. And he said his mom said you were—" He broke off and looked away from her.

It didn't take much imagination to guess what Alisha Paxton had said about her. She'd hated Piper since high school. While most people in the area knew and liked Piper, there were a few exceptions, Alisha being a prominent one.

She didn't force him to repeat any more. "Do you know what those words mean?"

He shrugged. "Yeah."

Did he really, she wondered, or did he know a garbled version of the true meaning? Probably the latter. "We'll talk about it when you get home from school."

When the principal returned, Piper informed her what had happened. Janie nodded. "Yes, I was afraid it was something like that." Turning to the still-defiant child, she said, "Cole, even if someone does something they shouldn't, like call you names, it doesn't make it right to hit them."

"But they said—" he started hotly.

"Fighting isn't allowed."

"Who cares?" Now he was only a small, sulky boy instead of a defender of his mother's honor.

"Tell Mrs. Settle you won't fight again."

He shot his mother a fulminating look, but he muttered, "Okay. But he'd better not call my mom names, either."

"I'll have a talk with him," Janie said. "You may go to the nurse now, and then back to class."

After he left, Janie covered Piper's hand with hers. "I'm so sorry, Piper. I know how hard this is on you."

"It just hit the papers this morning and look what's already happened." Piper passed a hand over her forehead. "Thanks, Janie. I've got to go home and figure out what I'm going to tell Cole."

"He's a good kid, Piper. He's never been in trouble before. That's why I'm not suspending him, but I'll catch flak for it."

"I know you will and I appreciate it, I really do. Usually Cole isn't a fighter."

A smile flickered across Janie's face. "He was defending you."

Piper buried her face in her hands. After a minute she looked up and said, "How am I going to explain it to him?"

"If I knew an easy answer I'd tell you, but I'm afraid there isn't one. Just do the best you can. It's all any of us can do." She studied Piper a moment and added, "Honey, it will blow over again, these things always do. Keep your chin up."

"Thanks, I'll try." But by the time she got home, Piper was no closer to having an answer than when she'd left.

Had she really been foolish enough to think she wouldn't have to tell Cole about his father? Piper thought later that afternoon. If she'd listened to Eric—No, that was the problem. She'd listened to him and now her son was suffering because of it.

Cole took his sandwich cookie and pried it apart,

dipping one side in his milk. Piper wondered if things like that were inherited; she'd never eaten her cookies that way. Maybe Roger had. That was a frightening thought. She didn't want Cole to be anything like Roger Griffin.

"Billy said I'm a bastard 'cause I don't have a dad. Is that true?" Cole's blunt question interrupted her train of thought. His eyes were on her, the unblinking, unflinching stare of a child who wants the answers.

"You have a father. He just doesn't live with us."

"Billy asked me what my dad was like. Why haven't you ever told me about him?"

"I should have," she admitted with difficulty. "But this is something that's hard for me to talk about."

"Why doesn't my dad live with us?" Relentlessly, as only a small child can, he pursued the topic with single-minded fervor.

"Because we're not married." Her stomach hurt. She wondered if she'd get through this talk without having a nervous breakdown.

"Oh, you mean like divorced," he said matter-of-factly.

"No, we weren't married."

That comment didn't seem to register. "Why doesn't he want to know me? Jamie's parents are divorced, but he still sees his dad."

"Your father and I were never married, Cole. It's different from when you get divorced."

Puzzled, he asked, "You mean you had me when you weren't married?"

"Well . . ." What could she say but the truth? "Yes."

"But that's wrong. It's wrong to have babies when you're not married. Why did you do that if you knew it was wrong?"

Piper spread her hands helplessly. "Sometimes people make a mistake—" Horrified, she cut herself off. All his life, she had been careful not to lead Cole to believe that she thought of him as a mistake. Because she didn't. She couldn't imagine her life without her son.

Surprisingly, he didn't say anything, but she knew he'd caught it. He just hadn't digested it yet. In the vain hope she might salvage something, she rushed on. "A lot of people think it's wrong, that's true. But sometimes two people have a baby and for some reason they can't get married. That's what happened to me." How did you explain shades of gray to a child who only thought in black and white?

"Why didn't you get married? You're s'posed to be married to have a baby. Aren't you?" His brown eyes gazed at her, imploring at the same time they accused.

Piper glanced away, biting her lip until she could feel the pain. This was worse, much worse, than she'd imagined. How could she tell him she couldn't have married Roger, even if he'd been willing? How was she supposed to tell her son that he was a result of her liaison with a married man? It wouldn't matter a damn to Cole that she hadn't known Roger was married, that she'd never known what kind of man he was until it was too late.

"Your father didn't want to marry me."

"Why?" Cole's voice rose in agitation. "He didn't want to marry you 'cause of me? That's why?"

"No!" She stretched out her hand toward him, but he drew back, still staring at her accusingly. "Cole, that's not true. He didn't want to get married because he didn't love me. It had nothing to do with you."

"But what about me? Didn't he love me, either?" His voice shrilled, his chest heaved. His small fists clenched in anguish.

Roger wouldn't even acknowledge him—another thing she'd never tell him. "It wasn't like that, honey. I love you so much I wanted you all to myself." Even to her it sounded lame.

"No, you're lying!" Cole shouted. "My daddy didn't want me, and you don't either! You said I was a mistake! You *said* it! I bet you wish you'd never had me!" He tore out of the house at top speed.

Piper ran to the door in time to see Cole dash across the pasture with Jumbo in lumbering pursuit. She didn't follow, deciding instead to send Charlie after him. His great-grandfather could get Cole to listen better than anyone. But listen to what? Six years old, she thought. So young, so impressionable. And right now she knew he felt like he couldn't depend on anyone.

Her son hated her. Burying her face in her hands, she gave in to the scalding, bitter tears of regret and misery. She'd never told Cole a thing about his father and then suddenly she hit him not only with his illegitimacy, but the fact that she thought he was a mistake. She'd done the one thing she'd sworn never to do and made him doubt his self-worth. Because she'd been afraid and had selfishly avoided telling him the truth.

TWELVE

Four days had passed since the story hit the papers. To Eric it felt like a year. He dialed Piper's number, hoping to pass directly to her the information he'd just received from Dave.

A gruff voice answered after the third ring. "Yeah."

"Charlie?" Of course it was Charlie. Piper hadn't answered the phone in days. "It's Eric." Charlie grunted. Eric figured that was as good as it was going to get, grateful he hadn't hung up. "I need to talk to Piper."

Charlie hooted. The old coot actually hooted at him. "Sorry, Doc. She don't want to talk to you."

Eric ground his teeth but managed not to yell at the old man. "Then you're going to have to talk to me. It's important. I've got some information and I might be able to help her."

"We-ll," Charlie drawled. "Start talking."

"No, I need to see you in person."

Charlie sighed. "I'd better come see you. Sam's sworn to take the shotgun to you if he sees your face around these parts. Myself, I'm partial to a good fistfight, but Sam's always been hot off the griddle. 'Course, Gus said the same thing, but he cain't shoot nearly as well as Sam."

Very subtle, Charlie. "Whenever you can get here," Eric said.

Half an hour later Charlie stomped into Eric's office. "What's so all-fired important?" he demanded.

The old rancher didn't look like he'd be easy to placate, Eric thought, but he'd expected that. "Thanks for seeing me."

"Talk quick."

"Piper still won't see me."

"Reckon so. Said something about a low-down, lying, conniving, no-good sonofabitch who makes a snake in the grass look like good news. You're about as welcome around our place as a rattlesnake in a prairie-dog town, Doc."

"I didn't leak that story, Charlie. A temporary clerk at Dave's clinic did it and she's been fired."

Charlie took a seat. "Don't matter much who leaked it. What matters is my little girl's life is being made a misery."

"Dave and I are doing everything we can to get the story dropped. I've been going crazy since this happened. She hasn't said a word to me, not one." Wearily, Eric leaned his hips against the front of his desk and shoved his hand through his hair. "I need to see her." More than a need, it was an obsession. "I've got to talk to her."

Unimpressed, Charlie cracked his knuckles. "Well, what do you want me to do about it?"

"Get her to see me." Eric stuffed his hands in his pockets and scowled at him.

The old man shook his head, a half smile hovering on his lips. "Not a chance, Doc. Not a dog's chance."

Damn the old coot, Eric thought. He was enjoying how miserable Eric was. "You don't understand, I've got to talk to her," he repeated. "We were seeing each other before all this happened. Hell, we've been seeing each other for weeks. I miss her." He waved his hand in the air. "I care about her. And I care about Cole too. Talk to her for me, Charlie."

Considering him from under bushy brows, Charlie stared at Eric for a long moment. Finally he spoke. "Cole came home from school that first day with a split lip and black eye. Kid called him a bastard. And you can guess what they called his mama. Natcherly, Cole up and busted him one. He wasn't sure what the words meant, but he's a smart kid. He knows when he's being insulted. Now, I wonder whose door she's laying that at?"

His, obviously. Eric spread his hands. "If I could stop it, or change it, don't you think I would?"

"She's not ready to talk to you, Doc. Maybe won't ever be."

He dragged his hand through his hair again. "How did Cole handle it?"

" 'Bout like you'd expect. Didn't understand a lot of the talk. Piper tried to explain it to him. Try tellin' a six-year-old that his daddy didn't want him and that you weren't married when you had him."

Eric winced. "What did he do when she told him?"

"Yelled at his mama and ran off. A while later I found him and talked to him some. He'll be okay. Maybe."

"God, I hate it that he's going through this. I wish there was something I could do for him."

Charlie snorted. "Well, you mighta thought of that before you talked Piper into giving that remedy to your friend."

"I didn't expect anything like this to happen."

"Piper told you it would. You should've listened to her."

He was right, dammit. Dead right. "Has Kimberly been any help?" Eric asked.

"Kimberly called up screeching the next day. Says she's talking to people. All I know is those reporters are still hanging around." The old man's shoulders shook as he chuckled. He laid a booted foot across one knee and put his hand on the other. "The last reporter who stuck his head in where it didn't belong has a dent the size of the Rio Grande Valley in his head. Piper beaned him with a clay pot. Always did have a good aim."

"I want to help her."

Bushy eyebrows drew together. "Piper needs a man who'll love her enough that her past won't matter to him."

Eric shoved himself away from his desk to pace the room. "I don't give a damn about her past. She knows that." Didn't she?

Charlie regarded him steadily. "Doc, right now the only thing she knows is that you wanted to sleep with her."

Eric stopped pacing and stared at him.

"That's nothing new and nothing unusual either," Charlie went on. "Piper's a grown woman now, old enough to decide what she wants. But hell, son," he said scornfully, "she needs more than that. If that's all you're after, she's better off without you."

"Damn you, Charlie, that's not all it is."

"Coulda fooled me. I never heard any talk about love or marriage. The way it looks to me, either you love her or you get out of her life and let her get on with it."

"Of course I love her!" Eric shouted. "For God's sake, do you think I'd be standing here humiliating myself if I didn't?"

Charlie grinned and sat back. "No need to shout, Doc," he said mildly. "I'm not deaf yet."

Hands fisted and his chest still heaving, Eric glared at him. His eyes narrowed. "Are you happy now?"

"Reckon so," he stated with a satisfied nod of his head. "Somebody had to push you to see it."

"I've known it for weeks. But it's not going to do me a bit of good if she won't even cross my path."

"You mighta known it but you haven't told her. What were you waiting for, son?"

Eric shook his head wearily and ran his hand over his brow. "What does it matter? It's too late."

Charlie grunted. "Give her some time, she'll come around. If she loves you, that is." He rose and stomped over to the door. Turning, he looked Eric over. "Guess you'll just have to be patient, Doc. See you around."

The next day, Eric's doorbell rang. He couldn't stop the brief, futile stab of hope that it might be Piper. He opened his door to see Cole standing on his doorstep, clutching something in his hands that appeared to be wiggling. Taking a closer look, Eric realized it was a horned toad.

Solemnly, the little boy gazed at him, his brown eyes looking too large for his face. "Can I come in?"

"Sure." He stepped back and let him enter. "What's going on, Cole?"

"My horny toad's sick. I know you said you couldn't fix animals, but—" He hung his head and didn't say anything else.

Eric squatted down and took the toad from him. It looked like a small, flat pineapple, just exactly like he'd expect a horned toad to look. Its skin felt rough, which from what he could remember from his youth, was normal. Small, beady eyes blinked at him.

"What's wrong with him?"

"Won't eat," Cole mumbled.

"What have you been trying to feed him?" He didn't believe for a minute that was why the boy was there, but he'd allow him to get to the real reason in his own time.

"Bugs, grass. You know, stuff." Shrugging, Cole looked away. "But he won't eat anything."

"Maybe he's just not hungry," Eric ventured, trying to keep the conversation going. His knees hurt; he wasn't used to squatting for long periods.

"I think he's sad," Cole said, the hint of a tear shining in his eye. "Nobody—" His voice broke and he continued, "Nobody wants him."

Looking into Cole's dirt-streaked face, Eric recognized the pain in his eyes. "I don't know a lot of animal medicine, but I do know that sometimes their owners can help them because they can tell us things that the animals can't."

In a quiet little voice Cole said, "His daddy hates him. His daddy ran away 'cause he hated him." Tears welled up in his eyes and spilled down his cheeks. "His mom doesn't want him neither."

Eric put his hand on the little boy's shoulder and squeezed. "Are you sure about that?"

Cole nodded mournfully and managed to stop crying after a moment.

Unable to kneel any longer for fear his circulation would be cut off, Eric rose. "How did you get here?" It was too much to hope that Piper had brought him, but he found himself hoping nonetheless.

"Lynn brought me. She'll be back."

Eric wondered how Lynn had known where to drop Cole, then he realized Effie must have told her his address. Effie would do anything for Cole. Even if she was almost as mad at Eric as everyone else.

"Come on." Gently, Eric prodded Cole along toward the kitchen. "Maybe some cookies will help."

"Maybe. What kind?" Cole asked with a little more interest, setting his pet on the floor.

"Gingersnaps." Eric picked him up and set him on the table so that he was nearer eye level.

"I like chocolate better." Cole started to swing his leg.

Eric grinned. "Me, too, but this is all I have." He watched the boy munch on a cookie. Though he was still upset, he seemed a little calmer now. "Would it help if I talked to your mom?"

Violently, Cole shook his head. Through his mouthful of cookie he said, "My mom's real mad at you. I heard her talking to Grandpa."

"Yeah. She's upset." The epitome of understatement. Detested him was more like it. He didn't want to imagine what she'd been saying to Charlie.

"Is that why you haven't been to see me?"

Eric lifted his shoulders in a gesture of defeat. "It's not because of you. Your mom—" How to put this delicately? Your mom hates my guts wouldn't cut it. Eventually he settled on the basic truth. "Your mom doesn't want to see me right now."

Lower lip protruding, Cole fixed Eric with an earnest, unblinking gaze. "Are you sure?"

What was this? "She's made it pretty clear that she doesn't want me around." It was all he could do to remember who he was talking to and not make his own feelings about the absurdity of Piper's reaction clear.

"I thought maybe . . ." Cole's voice trailed off, then he started again. "Maybe it was 'cause of me."

His conversation with Charlie came back to him. It didn't take much insight to realize what was going on in the kid's mind. "I've missed seeing you, Cole. I always have a good time with you." He grimaced and scratched his neck, struggling for the right words. "You see, I didn't mean to, but I did something that hurt your mom and she's still upset with me." It stuck in his craw to admit it, but he had hurt her, intentionally or not.

"What did you do?" Cole watched the horned toad hop across the kitchen floor.

"It's kind of complicated," Eric said, smiling wryly. "But you and I are still friends, okay?"

Perceptively, Cole said, "You're mad at Mom too.

Just like she's mad at you. Are you mad at her 'cause she did something bad?"

Eric laid a hand on the boy's shoulder. "She didn't do anything bad. Why do you say that?"

"She had me when she wasn't married. That's bad."

More problems at school, Eric wondered, or the same one stemming from his talk with his mother? "Some people think so, but I don't."

"Why not?"

Eric sighed and squeezed Cole's shoulder before letting go. "It's easy to say somebody's good or somebody's bad. But most people are like your mom, or like me, and they make mistakes. You're that way, too, aren't you? Don't you make mistakes sometimes?"

"I guess," he mumbled, hanging his head.

"Your mom was real young when she had you. But she wanted you, even though she knew some people would say bad things about her. Do you know why she wanted you so much?"

"No." The boy looked up at him.

Eric took hold of his chin and said clearly, "Your mom had you because she loved you. She loves you a lot, Cole."

"Huh," he snorted, jerking his head away. "She said I was a mistake. That means she doesn't want me."

"She didn't mean that. At least, not the way it sounded. You say the wrong thing sometimes, don't you?"

"Sure, but—"

Eric interrupted. "Your mom's just like you. She's your mom, and a grown-up, but inside she's a lot like you." He didn't know how to explain that parents weren't perfect. He didn't have any kids, for God's sake. How was he to know what to tell Cole? Besides that, it grated on him to have to defend Piper, at least right now when he was still hurting from her repeated rejections. But Cole shouldn't suffer because of his own bruised ego.

"Your mom loves you," he repeated. "Remember that."

Suddenly, Cole reached out and put his arms around his waist and hugged him. Eric suspected he was silent because he didn't want Eric to know he was crying again. So he patted Cole's back and soothed him, and wished that he had someone to help *him*.

Not again, Piper thought, hearing a commotion outside. She looked out the window to see Gus and Jumbo taking care of the latest nosy newsman, who rested flat on his back in the gravel drive with Jumbo's huge paws planted on his chest. The dog's big, bushy tail wagged happily and she could hear him bark every time the man tried to rise.

Wait a minute. Unless she was mistaken, the man currently lying underneath Jumbo was Dr. Dave Burson. Great place for him, she thought, but went to rescue him nonetheless. She strolled slowly across the drive, savoring his discomfort, listening to him shout at Gus.

"Dammit, old man," Dave yelled, "I'm not a reporter. Ask Piper if you don't believe me. And get this misbegotten mongrel off me."

She parked a fist on her hip and looked down at him.

"Dave, what a surprise. How's life been treating you lately?"

His beleaguered expression lightened. "Am I glad to see you. Tell this crazy old man I'm not a reporter. He wants to take a shotgun to me. And this dog must weigh a hundred pounds."

"More." She shook her head. "Do you think it's wise for me to tell him who you *really* are?"

If possible, his face turned even redder. "I've been trying to apologize for days now. Let me tell you what's happened."

"Missy, you want I should get the shotgun?" Gus asked.

"No, Gus, I don't think that will be necessary. Dr. Burson will leave peacefully, I'm sure."

"Burson?" he repeated incredulously. "The one what brung them dang reporters down on us?" The old man drew himself up to his full height, all five feet four inches of it. "That no-account, lyin', deceivin' friend of that other no-good varmint?" Gus's voice rose as he fairly quivered with indignation.

"That's the one," she said, grinning.

"Mister, you're either awful brave or awful stupid," Gus told Dave. "Why, if I'da been Sam you'd be pickin' buckshot out of your butt right now."

"Piper, please," Dave begged, "get this damn dog off me so we can talk."

She stroked her chin and smiled. "It's petty of me, but I like seeing you lie there in the dirt. After all, your little leak has landed me back in the dirt of the headlines one more time."

"You're acting like a child. At least hear me out."

"Oh, all right," she muttered, tugging on Jumbo's collar. Reluctantly, he allowed her to pull him away.

"Thank you." Dave sat up. "Could we discuss this in a civilized manner? Inside?" He eyed Gus and Jumbo with disfavor.

Piper sighed. "Come on, then. But I warn you, Dave, I'm not feeling very charitable toward you." She led him inside to the living room and sat, waving a hand at a chair. "Ten minutes. Start talking."

"A temporary employee leaked the story."

"Tell me something I don't know. Eric told Grandpa that yesterday." She gazed at him unhelpfully.

Clearing his throat, he tried again. "She's been fired. Eric and I have been doing everything we can to establish that the news is unverified and your remedy isn't a major discovery. I think we've succeeded. Have you read the recent articles?"

"Are you crazy? I haven't looked at a paper since all this blew up. Why would I want to read more garbage about myself?"

"The publicity isn't good for me either. This sort of thing makes me look like a quack. The clinic's important, Piper. So is the research."

She crossed her legs and leaned back in the chair. "Time's running out," she reminded him, checking her watch.

"I realize there's no possible way to make up for the pain we've inadvertently caused you, but—"

"Do you have any idea what it was like to have my past dragged out and splashed all over the papers again? As if it wasn't bad enough the first time it happened."

"Well, no, I—"

"Cut to the chase. Why are you here?"

"First to apologize. You wouldn't let me over the phone, and besides, I felt like it should come in person."

"Fine, you've apologized." She started to rise.

"Wait! The formula is much more important than we've led the press to believe. Research is progressing on its effect as an additive in the impotence injection. Preliminary findings indicate that it might be of use."

She stood, gazing at him ironically. "Whoopee. That should make you happy. Now that you've told me, you can go."

"This is going to help a lot of people. It's important. More important than your discomfort over the publicity."

"Discomfort?" She laughed bitterly. "Tell that to my son when the other kids call him a bastard. This wasn't exactly the way I wanted him to learn about his paternity."

Dave winced and stood too. "Look, I can't undo it, and I can't blame you for taking your anger out on me. Even though I didn't leak it myself, it's my responsibility. But why are you taking it out on Eric? You won't even see him, will you?"

She strode over to him and jammed her finger into his chest. "Don't you dare come in here and talk to me about Eric Chambers. If it weren't for him, I wouldn't be in this mess."

"You gave him permission to send the formula to me," Dave reminded her. "Somehow I doubt he beat it out of you."

Piper turned her back on him. "Go away, Dave. You make me tired."

"You're angry because you did the right thing and it came back to haunt you. The old saw—no good deed goes unpunished—is applicable in this case. But it was still the right thing to do. You can't blame Eric for that. Ask yourself this, Piper. Who are you hurting by this behavior?" He regarded her critically. "Eric? Sure. But you're hurting yourself just as much." Dave walked to the door. "Give him a chance, Piper."

"Tell Eric it didn't work."

"He didn't ask me to talk to you. But maybe he's better off without you. That's a pretty hard-line unforgiving attitude you've got. Eric sure doesn't need that."

"You'd be unforgiving, too, if your life had been ruined."

"It will pass. Publicity like this always does. You'll be a nine-day wonder and then the press will move on. And you'll be alone because you were too damn stubborn to admit that you were wrong to blame Eric." He put his hand on the doorknob.

"Of course you'd think that. You're his friend."

Dave released the knob and turned around to stare at her. She could see that he was angry, but that only made her own anger more potent. Who was he to be angry with her?

"Yes, I am his friend, and you need a friend too. I'll just give you the benefit of my advice, even though I know you won't listen. That train's gone by, Piper. Get on with your life and forget about your past. You're the only one who can't let it go." On those words he stalked out the door.

For an instant she wished she had something to

throw at his head, but she had to acknowledge that Dave had made several good points. Eric hadn't leaked the news and although he'd encouraged her, he hadn't forced her to give Dave the remedy. He had let her make that decision on her own, and when it backfired, she had blamed him. Because it was easier to blame him, to be angry with him, than to admit that this disaster had made her unworthiness all the clearer. She had deliberately fed her anger, hoping it would help her forget Eric. It hadn't worked.

THIRTEEN

Eric smiled at the woman sitting across from him, wishing he could think of something to say. Too bad Virginia and Randy hadn't been able to come with them. Odd, he thought, how they had backed out at the last minute, leaving him with nothing to do but offer to take Virginia's cousin to dinner.

Without doubt, Marie was pretty. Beautiful, really. And she seemed very pleasant. But the problem wasn't Marie, it was him. Beautiful or not, he didn't want to be with her. He wanted Piper, dammit.

He glanced at the doorway of the restaurant. The big blond man standing in it looked familiar. Greg McKinnley, he realized a moment later. When McKinnley moved aside, Eric saw Piper. Of course. McKinnley had warned him that he'd be checking on her.

Piper looked around the room and froze when she saw Eric. He held her gaze for a long moment, gave her an easygoing wave, and turned back to Marie. Out of the corner of his eye he saw her lay a hand on McKinnley's arm, and they walked off to their table—directly in Eric's line of vision. He clenched his jaw.

"Is something wrong?" Marie asked.

"Not a thing." He flashed her another smile, and decided he'd be damned if he let Piper make him feel like a jealous fool. So he flirted with Marie and pretended no interest in Piper. McKinnley, dammit. If she wanted McKinnley, then she was welcome to him. Eric didn't need her.

"Isn't that Chambers?" Greg motioned with a wave of his large hand. "Over there with the pretty brunette."

"Oh." Piper pretended surprise. "I hadn't noticed."

Greg laughed good-naturedly. "Come on, Piper. Your eyes have been glued to that table since we walked in."

Had she been so obvious? "Okay, I might have glanced that way." It was over, so why shouldn't he go out with someone else? She was here with Greg. But that was different, she argued with herself. Why did she still have to be in love with Eric? He'd found somebody else to spend time with quickly enough.

"If it's any consolation," Greg said, "he's been staring at you too. Every time you look away, he looks this way."

"Maybe he's just uncomfortable."

"Maybe, but I doubt it. I thought you said it was over. Doesn't look like things are over to me."

"It's definitely over." Over and done with. Finished. And he was out with another woman to prove it.

Greg patted her hand. "I don't usually play the part

of the shoulder to cry on, but if that's what you need, I'm willing."

She smiled at him. No, Greg wasn't the sort women would usually cry on, he was more the type they'd cry over. No wonder, either. With looks, charm, and money, what more could a woman want? And he'd been so kind to her. "Thanks, but I think I'd rather try to forget it."

"Whatever you want." He sipped his wine, but he kept hold of her hand.

It was too late for her to have what she wanted. Pride was all she had left. She wasn't about to let Eric know he'd gotten to her. For at least half an hour she made sure not to look his way. When she finally risked a glance, she saw that he and his date had left. Visions of what they might be doing filled her mind until she wanted to scream.

Not long after that Greg took her home. "Didn't Chambers know how lucky he was?" he asked as he walked her to her door. "How could he let you go over some garbage the papers printed?"

She gave him a crooked smile. "You've got it wrong. I'm the one who called things off between us."

His arms crossed over his chest, he studied her. "I hate to say this—man, I really hate to say this—but it looks like you made a mistake."

"Why do you keep acting like I'm—like he—"

Greg pulled her into his arms and kissed her. Piper didn't resist. She desperately wanted to see if Greg was wrong and she was over Eric. It was a good kiss, a pleasant kiss, even a very skillful kiss, but it didn't do a thing for her.

He raised his mouth from hers and smiled wryly. "If you ever get over him, let me know." He muttered, "Damn. One more," and kissed her again, briefly, before releasing her.

"I'm sorry," Piper said.

"It's all right. I didn't figure I had a chance, but"—he shrugged—"it was worth a try."

She watched him leave, wondering why she couldn't feel about him the way he wanted her to. But, she thought with sudden insight, Greg might not be as interested in her if she was interested in him.

When Eric opened his door late that night, Piper was the last person he expected to see. It blew him away. He wondered if he were hallucinating. Then she spoke and he knew she was no illusion.

"Are you alone?" she asked, with a hard edge to her normally soft whiskey drawl.

Glancing down, he realized he wore his oldest jeans, faded at the stress points, with the top button undone. And nothing else. One corner of his mouth lifted. "What's wrong, Angel? Afraid you're interrupting something?"

"Am I?" She didn't return the smile.

"Not at the moment," he couldn't resist saying. He stepped aside and she stalked past him.

"I saw you tonight at dinner," she said.

"Yeah, I saw you too. So?" He walked over to lean a hip against the dining table and watch her.

"So I didn't know you'd already started dating."

It pleased him to hear the tightness in her voice,

because it meant she hadn't liked seeing him with another woman. "Why wait?" He shot her an astute look. "You were there with McKinnley. How long did it take him to find out we weren't an item anymore?"

"He didn't know until today. Tonight wasn't really a date."

"Business, was it?"

Piper flushed. "Obviously, your date wasn't business," she shot back.

"No, purely pleasure. Did you expect me to hang around like a lapdog waiting for you to throw me a crumb? Sorry to disappoint you, Angel, but that's not my idea of fun."

"This was a mistake," she said, starting toward the door.

Eric reached out and grabbed her arm. If she'd wanted to be with McKinnley, then why was she here now? He was damned if he'd let her go before he found out. "Why did you come?"

She said nothing, averting her eyes.

He could think of only one reason why she would have come. Because she didn't want McKinnley, she wanted him. And God knows, he wanted her too. He pulled her closer until she stood between his legs, and ran his hands up her back, slowly, sensually. "Tell me," he said softly.

His hands slid down over her bottom, and he pressed her against him, so he could feel her heat through the denim of his jeans. He could smell sex in the air, feel it in the quivering tension between them, and he knew she felt it too. But he wanted the words to come from her. "Why are you here?"

Her eyes closed and opened. Her gaze locked with his. "Because I missed you." Her voice was husky, low, the sound a seduction in itself. "I wanted so much to forget you, and I can't."

"God knows I can't forget you, either." He kissed her then, thrusting his tongue inside her mouth as it opened under his, the kiss exploding into a desire so intense that he burned with it. He could feel her going up in flames too. He swept her mouth with his tongue, engaging hers in an erotic rhythm so much like making love, he wasn't sure how long he could continue without completing the act.

Sliding his hands up under her dress, he caressed her hips, finding only a thin wisp of nylon . . . and Piper. He shoved her skirt up above her hips, settled her more firmly against him, and heard her indrawn hiss of breath when she realized he was already fully aroused.

"You'd better be sure about this, Angel, because you're not going to get a chance to change your mind."

She rocked her hips against his and pulled his mouth back to hers. With a muffled groan, he turned her around so that her hips rested against the edge of the table.

He jerked her blouse out of the waistband of her skirt and ran his hands up under it to rest below her breasts, to feel her smooth, warm abdomen rise and fall. Beneath the cotton bra, her nipples tightened. Her heart rate increased, her skin flushed. She was as ready as he was, or would be in moments. A shiver coursed through her as he massaged her breasts through soft cotton before flicking her bra open to expose her bare skin.

"Damn." Somewhere, he had a condom, but he

didn't want to stop to find it. He wanted to be inside her now, sooner than now. "Damn," he repeated. "Wait, I have to get something."

Her hands touched his zipper. "The pocket of my skirt," she said breathlessly, and slowly dragged the zipper down.

"You came prepared." He searched for the pocket in the crumpled material of her skirt. "You came here for this."

"Yes," she whispered.

His fingers closed around a small packet. "Good. Because I can't wait for the bedroom." He laid her back on the table, covering her nipple with his mouth, sucking deep and strong before he traced his tongue over to her other breast. She arched and groaned, her hands buried in his hair. He slid her panties off and all he could think was he had to have her now, right now. His fingers found the slick heat between her legs, and he only had to stroke her a few times before pushing her to the edge.

Sweet, hot sounds came from the back of her throat, and he knew there wasn't a chance in hell he could slow down or wait a minute longer. He barely managed to rip the packet open and protect her before he buried himself deep inside her and she wrapped her legs around his waist, raising her hips off the table to meet him thrust for thrust.

Had he ever felt like this? A burning frenzy, an almost crazed need for her that he'd never felt for another woman. Piper was as wild as he, taking him with the same nearly savage desire he took her. Then he felt her convulsing around him and he thrust again and again, hard and fierce and endlessly until he exploded deep within her.

Eric didn't know how long it was before he realized she lay underneath him on the table and he'd taken her like some kind of lunatic. But she wasn't upset. Her eyes were closed and the smile that curved her lips spoke of satiation. She opened her eyes and looked at him.

"Are you okay?" he asked.

"Better than okay," she said in a sexy murmur that made him want her again, right then, right there.

Reluctantly, he eased away from her, taking her hands in his to help her sit up. "Come on, let's go to the bedroom." He carried her in, laid her on the bed, and began to strip off the rest of her clothes.

"That woman you were with tonight," she said hesitantly. "Have you been dating her long?"

"Are you delicately trying to ask me if I've slept with anyone since you?" He jerked her blouse off, and she gasped.

"Have you?"

"You should have asked me that before now, Angel." With that, he flung her skirt to the side. He smiled. She was naked and waiting for him. He shouldn't still want her so much, but he did. "But no, I haven't."

"Aren't you going to ask me?" Her hand whispered over his chest and trailed down to his erection.

"No." Because if he didn't know the answer to that, then he didn't know Piper at all. He planted his knee between her legs and said, "Now be quiet and let me make love to you."

A long time later, she said, "I've got to go."

"Not yet." And he made love to her again.

❖———————❖

Late the next day, with her hands full of a large, muddy orchid, Piper felt an arm slide around her waist.

"Hi," Eric said, dropping a kiss on her ear. "If you'd put that plant down, I could find out something I've been wondering about all day." His lips trailed down her neck.

Her stomach did a somersault at the sound of his voice and the feel of his lips on her skin. She turned, and he pulled her into his arms and kissed her. She had the feeling that in about thirty seconds the door would be locked and she'd find out what it was like to make love standing up in a greenhouse.

She managed to pull back and give a shaky laugh. "You don't believe in starting off slow, do you?"

He smiled, but he looked serious, sexy, and appealing with his hair falling over his brow. "Will you marry me?"

Just like that. Out of the blue. Totally flabbergasted, she stared at him. "M-m-marry you?" she stammered.

"Yes, marry me." His eyes weren't green now, they were deep gray and fathomless.

There was no mistake, he'd asked her to marry him. "Why?"

He looked a little amused at her blunt question. "Because I love you. You must have figured that out by now."

Slowly, she shook her head. "No, I hadn't."

Eric took her hand and kissed it, then kissed her gently on the lips. "I love you and I want you to marry me."

She wanted to say yes and fling her arms around his neck and not worry about a thing, but she couldn't. He didn't trust her. He desired her, he *thought* he loved her, but he didn't trust her.

"You've never mentioned marriage before."

"I'm mentioning it now. What's wrong? Is it Cole? You know I want him, Piper. I want to be his father."

She took her hand from his, desperately trying to put a distance between them. "It's not Cole. But I can't marry you."

Frowning, he searched her face. "Then what was last night about? That meant something to me, Piper, and I thought it meant something to you."

"It did. But Eric, you don't trust me. Last night you were afraid to ask me if I'd been with anyone else. Admit it."

"I didn't ask you because I wouldn't have made love to you if I'd thought you had been with anyone else. Because I do trust you, not because I don't."

"We've never talked about San Antonio."

"What's to talk about? McKinnley jerks my chain, that's all San Antonio was about. You said you weren't involved with him, so there's no problem."

"How can you ask me to marry you when you think I'm a carbon copy of your ex-wife?"

"If I thought that I wouldn't want to marry you." Angrily, he spun away, pacing a few steps before turning back to her. "Okay. Yes, I'll admit some old fears surfaced that night, but I've had time to come to terms with my feelings. Any qualms I might have had just don't exist any longer. You're not Dawn."

He paused and walked back to her. "But this isn't

about me. This is about you. You can't trust a man, you can't trust me, because of something that happened over seven years ago. Dammit, I'm not paying for another man's sins. Just because that son of a bitch lied to you and manipulated you doesn't mean I will."

"Can you honestly tell me you've forgotten what I did?"

"Hell, yes, I can forget it, but you can't. You'll never let yourself forget it. You'd much rather wallow in guilt."

She hadn't meant to make him furious. "Why can't we—Why can't things go on like they are, at least until . . ."

He walked over to one of the benches and leaned back against it, crossing his arms over his chest. "It's not enough. Not anymore. I want more. More than just the sex. It's great sex, Angel, but I want something else too."

When she started to speak he cut her off with a ruthless gesture. "Let me finish, Piper. I want to marry you, be a father to Cole, have some more kids with you. If you don't think we can have that, then it's over. I won't settle for less."

That's what he'd be doing if he married her, she thought. Settling for less. And she couldn't let him do it. "Then it's over. Because I can't marry you."

Anger followed the pain and disbelief that darkened his face. "You're serious," he said, his voice harsh.

"Yes." She turned her back and heard the door slam. Bowed her head and let the tears fall.

FOURTEEN

The sky dripped a gray mist, sullen and leaden as Eric's mood. Unable to sleep, he'd come in early hoping to get some paperwork done, but it had been a useless gesture since he couldn't concentrate on anything but his personal disaster. Over and over he asked himself why he'd let Piper manipulate that final scene between them when losing her was the last thing he wanted.

His phone rang. He reached for it, preferring an emergency to his thoughts. "Chambers."

"Eric. I hoped you were in already."

"Piper." He felt a brief surge of hope before he realized why she must be calling. "Is Charlie having trouble?"

"No, Cole's really sick. I think it's the flu."

"He had the flu shot."

"I know, but I still think it's flu. Could I bring him in?"

"Bring him. I'll be here." However much he might have wanted Piper's visit to be an excuse to see him, he knew it wasn't. She'd sounded far too worried for him to believe that.

A short time later, after examining Cole, Eric was concerned himself. Probably the flu, he decided, but it must be a strain resistant to the vaccine, because Cole appeared to be getting a full-blown case of it.

Over the next few days, Eric talked to Piper several times, but Cole only grew worse. Her frantic call the afternoon of the third day sent him out to the ranch.

As Piper watched Eric examine Cole, she reminded herself that the flu made people very ill. Cole's cheeks were flushed, hectic with color, and his eyes held the glazed look common when running a high fever.

"Feel pretty bad, huh, buddy?" Eric said, laying a hand on Cole's forehead. "When did you last take his temperature?" he asked Piper.

"Just a little while ago. It went down after I bathed him. To 103.8."

"No wonder he feels lousy." Helping Cole to a seated position, he pulled up his nightshirt and placed his stethoscope on the boy's chest. Eric wore his professional face, the one that gave no hint of what he was thinking. His expression, or lack of it, made him look like a stranger. But that's what they were now, Piper thought. Strangers.

Finally he finished and let Cole lay back down. "Tell me again how this started out," he said to her.

"Like a bad cold that just kept getting worse. We haven't slept through the night in days."

"Any nausea, vomiting?" He ran his hand over Cole's abdomen and pressed on it in different areas.

"No vomiting. He's complained on and off of his stomach hurting, but he does that every time he's sick."

Eric frowned. "Does your stomach hurt now, Cole?" He pressed down again, on his right side. "Does it hurt there?"

"Hurts all over." Cole's voice was weak. "My head hurts too. Make it go away," he said querulously.

"It's the flu, isn't it?" she asked, but she knew it wasn't.

Eric stood and put a hand on her shoulder. "It acts more like the flu than anything else, but . . . Just make him as comfortable as you can."

She saw him to the door. "You're worried, aren't you? What is it?"

Surprising her, he pressed his hand against her cheek and smiled ruefully. "Doctors are funny about their families. I can't just turn off my feelings for him. I'm going to go back to work, but I'll be back later. Call me if you need me."

Piper watched him leave. She sensed there was something he wasn't telling her, but she knew he wouldn't open up. He'd said he couldn't turn off his feelings for Cole. What about his feelings for her?

Cole called to her and she sat beside him again, holding his hand and telling him stories in the vain hope he might forget how wretched he felt.

"I'm putting him in the hospital," Eric told Piper that evening after he'd examined Cole again.

Piper didn't argue. She didn't need a thermometer to know that Cole's fever was extremely high. The heat radiated in waves from his skin. Eric's grim face when he examined Cole had only solidified her fears. "What do you think it is?"

"I don't know." His voice was flat and unemotional. His professional voice. She wanted to yell at him for his calm, yet at the same time she was intensely grateful for it.

"Don't you even have an idea?"

"We're taking him in so we can run tests, Piper. Until then we won't know. Speculating doesn't do a bit of good."

Two hours and all sorts of tests later, she still knew nothing. Eric came in to stand by Cole's bed and frown at him while he slept restlessly.

She was sick with worry and sick to death of evasions. "What are you testing him for? Tell me, dammit. I'm his mother, I have a right to know."

He turned his attention away from Cole to look at her. "Giving you a diagnosis when I'm not certain will only make you worry unnecessarily."

She dragged him away from the bed. "Just tell me, Eric."

He sighed and glanced over at Cole before he met her eyes. "I've got a suspicion that it might be hantavirus."

"Hantavirus?" Her eyebrows drawn together, she stared at him. "The mystery disease that was in the papers recently?" Oh, God, she remembered now. Nauseated, she shut her eyes. "That's the disease that killed those people in New Mexico."

He hesitated. "There have been some deaths associated with it."

"Oh, my God." Hantavirus. The only thing she knew about it was what she'd read in the paper. And all of those people had died. "Is it—is it always fatal?" she managed to ask.

"Good God, no." He put his arm around her and hugged her. "I shouldn't have told you until I was sure. We don't even know that he has it."

"It—it might not be that?" How could Cole have a disease she'd hardly even heard of?

"It could be another virus. Maybe a strain of flu that's resistant to the vaccine."

"When will we know?" She turned and clutched at the lapels of his coat, her fingers digging into the fabric, while her eyes were fixed on his, imploring him for answers. "Tonight?"

He shook his head and covered her hand, patting it consolingly. "It will take a day or so for the lab results to come in. We'll just have to wait."

Her gaze turned blank, her fingers loosening and slipping away. "Wait?" She closed her eyes. "Eric, I'm scared."

"I could be wrong."

She opened her eyes and looked at him. "You could be wrong," she repeated tonelessly. "What happens if . . ." She couldn't finish the sentence.

"He's here in the hospital, Piper. They're equipped to deal with it if he should become worse."

Piper took that for what comfort she could, which was damned little.

———❧————❧———

Two days later, Eric stared at Cole's lab report. Positive for hantavirus. The report had come in while he was making rounds. He held it a moment, looking for the possibility of error, but there was none. Hantavirus, a disease that killed sixty percent of those who contracted it. Cursing, he threw the report on his desk.

Piper sat in a chair drawn up beside Cole's bed. The same place he saw her every time he went in. "Come take a break. I'll send Charlie or your mother in if you want."

She glanced up at him, her face drawn, exhaustion etched on it. "You know, don't you? You've gotten some test back."

"Come on, Piper. We don't need to discuss it in here."

He took her to one of the staff offices. She looked fragile, exhausted, scared to death. Knowing no way to soften it, he spoke bluntly. "It's hantavirus."

Her face paled. Her hands were gripped together so tightly, he could see her knuckles turning white. "Is he going to die?"

"No." There was no way he could guarantee that, but he couldn't face that possibility any more than Piper could. "No, he's not going to die."

"Those other people did."

"He won't die, Piper. He isn't exhibiting the worst symptoms, so we have to hang on to that for now." She went to him then, all of the fight drained from her. He held her and wished he could guarantee the outcome as he'd never wished for anything before.

As a physician he'd rarely felt more helpless. Hantavirus was a new disease without a prescribed course of treatment. There was a new drug available to treat certain strains of the disease, but until Cole worsened, Eric couldn't give it to him. All he could do was treat his symptoms and wait.

Piper held Cole's hand as he shifted restlessly on the hospital bed. She thought about all she'd gone through to have him. The publicity that had resulted from her liaison with Roger, the torment she'd endured from the press. It was worth anything she'd suffered to have this one small child to love. As she gazed down at him, she saw him gasp for breath. Within minutes he began turning blue. She hit the emergency button beside his bed.

An endless time later, Eric ran in with two nurses, took one look at Cole, and said, "Piper, wait outside." After that he ignored her, pushing her out of his way to get to her son, slapping an oxygen mask on him, and snapping out orders to the nurses. "Intubate him and then put him on the vent. Now!"

She waded in a quicksand, her mind mired in terror, ensnared by the grim reality of the sight before her. Immobile, she focused on her son's face. She heard nothing, saw nothing but Cole, lying deathly still. *Please, God, don't let him die.* Her breath let out in a sobbing gasp. A nurse led her to the door. She walked blindly into her grandfather's arms and laid her head on his chest. "Grandpa, what if he doesn't—"

"Hold on, girl. Cole's a Stevenson and we don't give up, so don't let me hear you talk that way. He'll pull through." He patted her back. For the first time in her memory she felt a tremor in her grandfather's hand.

"He has to, Grandpa. Oh, God, he has to."

They waited, each trying desperately to believe what they told each other. Interminable minutes later, Eric emerged from Cole's room, his face drawn and weary. "He's stable now. Go take a look at him and then let Charlie stay with him, Piper. After you see him I'll explain what we did."

So she went in and reassured herself that Cole was alive. Hooked up to a machine, but alive. She smoothed the hair on his head and thought about how unnaturally still he was. Cole, the child who always ran, lying motionless on a hospital bed.

"We've put him on the ventilator," Eric said when she came out. "I've started him on that new antiviral drug I told you about. The machine's helping him breathe, so that's good."

She felt herself losing it, but couldn't stop. "How can you say it's good when he has to be hooked up to a machine so he can breathe?" Tears ran down her cheeks and she beat her fists on his chest. "How can you say anything about this is good?"

Eric held her while she cried, unable to comfort her. She was right. Nothing about this was good. Ironically, he'd had to wait until Cole worsened, until the virus attacked his lungs, before he could take a more aggressive course of treatment. Now he was finally able to give Cole a drug prescribed for the particular strain of hantavirus that he had. A drug that might or might not help him.

Eventually Piper's tears slowed and she looked up at

him. His heart twisted at the fear in her eyes, tore with his inability to offer solace, to offer a solution.

"It's not your fault," she said. "I'm just so scared. So scared that he's going to die."

"I know, Angel, I know. It's okay. Yell at me if it helps."

"Eric, I can't lose him," she said, her fists clenched against his chest. "He's so young, he's only six years old."

She was counting on him for the answers, trusting him to save her son. And he was horribly afraid that he couldn't.

His arms tightened around her. More than he'd ever wanted anything in his life, he wanted to be able to tell her that Cole wouldn't die. But he couldn't do that. "He's stable." *For now.* "We should know in a day or two whether the new drug will help."

Striving to regain her composure, she sniffled and pulled away from him. "How long is he going to be hooked up to that machine?"

"As long as he needs it."

"How—Why were you here when it happened?"

"Luck. I'm here at the hospital to do my morning rounds, and your call came in while I was standing at the nurses' station."

"I'm glad you were here." She placed a hand on his arm and squeezed it. "I know the nurses would have handled it, but I'd much rather have you."

Again, he didn't know how to reply. "Go on back to him. I've still got rounds to do and some calls to make."

"Will you come back to see him later?"

He touched her cheek with his fingers. "Count on it." He gave her a last hug and left.

After that, Eric spent every spare moment on the phone to anyone who knew anything about hantavirus. Information was sketchy, treatment controversial—a potentially fatal disease that no one knew exactly how to treat. He did the best he could and prayed that Cole would come out of it. And he tried not to think about the consequences if his best just wasn't good enough.

All that day and most of the night, Cole remained on the ventilator. Sometime after midnight Eric came into Cole's room and found Piper asleep in the chair. He let her sleep while he examined the boy.

"Wake up, Angel."

Piper opened her eyes and looked at him. Smiling at her, he said, "You need to leave the room."

"Why?" She glanced at Cole, then sat up and rubbed sleep from her eyes.

"So we can take him off the machine. He's better, Piper. Cole's getting better." For the first time in days, Eric felt like he could breathe again.

Hope blazed in her eyes. "You're sure? He'll be all right?" She turned to look at her son again, her hand squeezing his spasmodically.

"His lungs are clearing, he's breathing on his own. The virus is weakening, the new drug is working. He should improve rapidly now." Though Cole wasn't totally out of danger, from what Eric had read, once the new drug took effect, the patient showed every likelihood of a full recovery.

She closed her eyes. "Thank God," she whispered. Reaching out, she took Eric's hand and cradled it against her cheek. "Thank you. When I thought I'd lose him . . . You can't know what it means to me."

His gaze held hers for a long moment. "Yes, I can. He might not be mine, Piper, but I love him too." He wished . . . What he wished wasn't going to happen. Not now, not ever. He would be Cole's doctor, never his father. Never Piper's husband.

"I know you do," she said, squeezing his hand. "I've got to tell Mother and Grandpa."

"Do that." His grin was weak, but he managed one. "Maybe your mother will quit terrorizing the nurses now."

From the doorway, she smiled at him. It was one of the most beautiful sights he'd ever seen.

"Oh, I doubt that, she's been enjoying it so. But I'll tell them."

FIFTEEN

From the moment he went off the ventilator, Cole recuperated rapidly. In a matter of days he left the hospital. It took him a little longer to return to full strength, but within a couple of weeks he was much as he'd always been, full of boundless energy and enthusiasm, an extremely active almost seven-year-old boy.

Piper took longer to recover than Cole did. Each day that passed helped her to forget, but she still thought it a miracle, every time she saw him running and playing. Memories of him lying motionless in the hospital, hooked up to a machine that breathed for him, never failed to evoke a fervent prayer of thanks.

Eric came by often, but he came to see Cole, not her. Piper wondered if he'd managed to get over her as easily as it seemed he had. While he was pleasant to her, he treated her as if she were an acquaintance and not the woman he'd asked to marry him. The woman who had turned him down and was now trying desperately to think of a way to get him back.

While Cole was so dangerously ill, Piper had

thought of nothing else. Every moment, waking and sleeping, had centered on her son and the hope that he would get well, the despair that he might not. But once he was on the mend, she had ample time for reflection. It didn't take her long to realize that she had been a fool to throw away her chance at happiness with Eric.

Every word that she had spoken, every word he had said to her came back to haunt her. Almost losing Cole had driven her to admit that Eric had been right. Her fear, her mistrust, her guilt were the problem, not Eric's mistrust. She knew now that he would never have asked her to marry him if he hadn't resolved his feelings, if he hadn't believed he could trust her.

And what had she done? What had she done when he told her that he loved her, that he loved her son and wanted them to be a family? She'd thrown it back in his face because she didn't trust herself. Eric wouldn't ask her again. It was up to her. If she wanted him, she'd have to fight for him.

The doorbell rang. Piper took a deep breath, wiped sweaty palms on her dress, and opened the door. "Come on in, Eric," she said, taking the wine he handed her. "I'm so glad you could come." Her voice sounded calm and confident, she thought, and wondered at herself.

He glanced around warily. "Where is everybody? The place is so dead I thought no one was home."

"They're all out. Until very late."

His eyebrows rose. "Didn't Cole—"

"I let you think I was asking you to dinner for Cole's sake." From under her lashes she sent him a mischievous look. "Because I knew you wouldn't turn him down." She watched his expression turn even warier. "Why don't you open the wine?" she asked, leading him to the kitchen.

He took the corkscrew, appearing to concentrate on the process of uncorking the wine. After pouring it, he handed her a glass. "You look very beautiful tonight."

She smiled and thanked him. It was the first personal thing he'd said to her since Cole's illness. She had worried that the midnight-blue dress with its low-cut neckline was a little too obvious, but he didn't appear to think so. His gaze, she noticed, had a tendency to drift to her cleavage. No, things might not be as hopeless as she'd feared.

Over a candlelit dinner they made light conversation. "Virginia told me she's pregnant again," Piper said when they were nearly finished. "That's wonderful, but I understand it had nothing to do with my remedy."

"Afraid not. We switched Randy's medications around and that solved the problem. But they're still working on your remedy as an additive."

"Yes, I know. Dave and I talked about it. He's very excited."

"If your formula increases the effectiveness of that injection, chances are the press will be on your case again."

"It's not important," she said, waving her hand airily.

"Not important?" He stared at her. "Since when?"

"Since Cole found out about his father. Now that he knows, the press can't hurt us anymore. You were right about that, Eric. I should have told him long ago."

"You did tell him."

"When it was nearly too late. I seem to have a problem with that, figuring things out when it's almost too late."

Eric didn't answer, but looked at her thoughtfully, his gaze fixed on her face.

"Bring your wine." She rose and walked to the couch, seated herself, and slowly crossed one leg over the other. "Sit beside me," she invited, patting the cushion. Her hand went to the neckline of her dress and began to fiddle with the buttons.

He crossed the room but didn't take the proffered seat. Instead he stood in front of her, his gaze traveling up the length of her legs, checking briefly at her cleavage, and continuing on to her face.

"I might get a call," he said. "For work."

She raised an eyebrow. "Effie told me you and Dr. Forrest were trading call nights and that the two of you had discussed forming a partnership. She assured me that you were off tonight."

Eric gave her a dirty look. She smiled blandly in return. "Have you ever been hunting, Angel?"

"Yes." Her cheeks dimpled. "Grandpa and Sam taught me."

He muttered something and said, "Did they teach you to stalk your quarry?"

"Mother taught me that," she said, and gave a gurgle of laughter.

He held his wineglass in his hand, regarding her silently. After a long scrutiny, he spoke. "Are you trying to seduce me, Piper?"

"Now what gives you that idea?" she asked, her fingers still on the buttons at her neckline.

He lifted a shoulder. "If it looks like it and feels like it, it usually is. And this sure as hell looks like it and feels like it."

"What if I was? Could I . . . still?" she asked, her voice husky, hesitant.

"Seduce me?" Once again, his gaze drifted over her. "In a New York minute."

She let out the breath she'd been unaware of holding. "Good," she said softly.

He finally sat beside her. "But I told you before, that's not all I want."

"I remember. I've had a lot of time to think about what happened. Cole's illness made me think about a lot of things. About loving and trusting and believing. Forgiveness. About being happy with what we have. I'm so lucky, so thankful, because I could have lost my son and I didn't. And that's because of you."

"It's not your gratitude that I want," he said harshly.

"But you have it. And you have something else too." She drew in a deep breath and reached for his hand. "You have my heart, Eric. If it's not too late."

He closed his eyes briefly, then opened them. "Do you trust me, Piper?"

"Will you believe me if I tell you yes? If I tell you that I was afraid to trust myself?"

His voice was deep, quiet. "I want to believe you."

"How could I trust myself when I wanted so desperately to have a normal home life—something I'd never had—that I never saw the signs of Roger's lies? When I found out the truth it nearly destroyed me, because I hadn't wanted to know. I'd been deliberately blind. And I couldn't risk that again, because of Cole."

"You thought I'd destroy you?"

"No, but I thought you'd realize I wasn't worthy of you, and that would destroy me. And, Eric, you didn't trust me, not at first."

"No, I didn't. Not totally." He reached out a hand to caress her cheek.

"When Neil told you—"

"At first it mattered. I won't try to pretend it didn't, because it did. But I was already falling in love with you." He took her hand, rubbing her palm with his thumb. "And later . . . Piper, I'd never have made love to you that night, I'd never have asked you to marry me if I hadn't trusted you."

"I know that now. Maybe I even knew it then, but I was scared. It wasn't until I faced losing my son that I understood the true meaning of fear. When I thought he would die, I saw how fragile our lives can be and what a fool I had been to throw away happiness. I realized I was punishing Cole, and myself, for a mistake I paid for years ago. And I didn't have to punish myself anymore. All I had to do was trust myself. I love you, Eric."

"Enough to let go of the past?"

"It's gone."

He pulled her into his arms and kissed her then, a seal and a promise. "I should give you a chance to think about it again, but I'm not going to. We're getting married. Soon."

"Yes. Very soon." She brought his head back down to hers.

Eric stopped her, framing her face in his hands. "I love you, Piper." He lowered his head to hers again, crushed her mouth underneath his.

"Mom!" Cole burst through the front door with his usual enthusiasm. "Jason's mom said—" He broke off, staring at the two of them. "Lynn said that you didn't want me to come get my game I forgot, but I knew you wouldn't mind. Do you?"

With her arms still around Eric's neck, Piper turned her head to glare at her son. "Yes. Your timing stinks, Cole."

"Huh?"

She dropped her arms. "Never mind. Just get the game and then go back to Jason's."

"Okay. They're waiting outside. Want me to ask them in?"

"No!" Piper said vehemently. "I want you to get your game and scram."

"Geez, Mom." He looked at them again and asked, "How come you were hugging each other?"

"Because we're getting married," Eric told him, grinning at Piper. "That's what people do when they decide to get married."

"You're gonna marry Eric?" Cole asked his mother.

"Yes. You don't mind, do you?"

He didn't answer her, but stared at Eric, his eyes big and questioning. "You're gonna be my dad?"

Eric nodded solemnly. "If you want me to be. That's what I want."

"Will you still play video games with me?"

"You bet." Eric grinned at Piper again.

"Is that all you think about?" she demanded of her son.

"But I like video games, Mom." Turning back to

Eric he said, "Maybe you can teach me football too. Mom can't play." He looked a little disgusted at that.

"Sure thing, sport." Eric held up his hand.

Cole ran to him and slapped it. "Way cool. I gotta go tell Jason." He headed for the door at a dead run.

"Wait a minute," Piper said. "Don't forget your game."

"Oh, yeah." Cole dashed off to his room, reappearing with the game a few minutes later.

"See you in the morning," Piper said, walking him out.

"I hope you plan on locking that door," Eric said.

"Definitely." She shook her head. " 'Way cool.' That's all he could think of?"

"Sounds good to me. Coming from a six-year-old, anyway."

He was looking at her with a glint in his eyes that she could see and translate from across the room.

"Don't take this wrong," he said, the timbre of his voice deepening, "but I don't want to talk about Cole right now."

"Did you have something else in mind?" she asked as she crossed the room to stand before him.

"I'll give you a hint. It's not talking."

She laughed as he pulled her down into his lap and kissed her. "So, you don't want me to talk?" She looped her arms around his neck and kissed his cheek.

"You can talk. As long as it's my name, said in that breathy little voice you get when—"

"Eric!" she interrupted, laughing. "Eric," she said again, in a different tone as his hand stole up her leg.

"That's the way," he said, and kissed her.

THE EDITORS' CORNER

Happy anniversary! No, not you—us! June 1997 marks the fourteenth anniversary of LOVESWEPT. Many of you have been with us since the inception of LOVESWEPT. For that, we thank you and we hope to continue our strong relationship with our loyal readers. Speaking of relationships, have we got some doozies for you! Our fourteenth anniversary lineup includes everything from corporate intrigue, pretend weddings, diamonds, and babies. (And not necessarily in that order!) Oh yeah, remember last month's editors' corner where we told you to keep an eye out for that "new, yet traditional look" in LOVESWEPT's future? Well, the future is now, baby!

With his company at stake as well as his heart, Rio Thornton must guard himself from the golden-eyed corporate princess Yasmine Damaron in **THE DAMARON MARK: THE HEIRESS,** LOVE-

SWEPT #838, by bestselling author Fayrene Preston. A trademark Damaron, Yasmine is very much in control of herself and her heart, but when she faces the fiercely masculine executive, the heat of his desire stuns and arouses her. She makes Rio an offer he can't refuse, insisting that she's only after his business, but Rio's heart is the soul of his business. Can he give his heart away without losing the one thing he needs most? With a story that's both sensual and charming, Fayrene Preston is back, in this latest installment of the Damaron series.

In Destiny, Texas, there is a force at work: a fortune-teller with mystical powers of foresight. However, in Karen Leabo's **BRIDES OF DESTINY: MILLICENT'S MEDICINE MAN**, LOVE-SWEPT #839, Millicent Whitney, a widow and expectant mother, refuses to believe that Dr. Jase Desmond is the one for her. She's already had the love of her life and now he's dead, leaving her with a baby on the way. Way out of his league, neurosurgeon Jase Desmond helps to deliver Millicent's baby and realizes that he's been denying himself for far too long. Can Jase teach Millicent that loving again isn't betraying a memory but opening her heart to new dreams? In this poignant love story of new beginnings and second chances, Karen Leabo explores the funny and tender side of starting over, with this last chapter of the Brides of Destiny series.

Suzanne Brockmann returns with another sexy and charming comedy in **STAND-IN GROOM**, LOVESWEPT #840. Chelsea Spencer has to get married in order to receive her inheritance, but the man she's chosen has just RSVPed his regrets. Suddenly she remembers the handsome (and interested) stranger who'd saved her from being mugged. When she offers Johnny Anziano the opportunity to make his dreams come true, Johnny jumps at the chance to get to know Chelsea, even if it includes marrying her first. Chelsea and Johnny's shaky alliance means a risky marital charade and a spirited romp that is irresistibly seductive and utterly romantic.

Fate. Faith. The laws of divine reciprocity. Drake Tallen has his own word to define the priceless gem he found: Justice. In **FLAWLESS**, LOVESWEPT #841, Drake knows that this perfect gem will lure Emery Brooks back home long enough for him to exact his sweet revenge on his almost-bride-to-be. Ten years ago, Emery had run from the small Indiana town to an empty life in Chicago. Now tasked with buying the gem from Drake, Emery must face the man she loved and left, but can she resist his dark desire and the memories too strong to deny? And can she do it without surrendering her heart for the perfect stone? Cynthia Powell's latest novel delivers one surprise after another in a story sizzling with sensual secrets.

Happy reading!

With warmest wishes,

Shauna Summers

Joy Abella

| Shauna Summers | Joy Abella |
| Editor | Administrative Editor |

P.S. Look for these Bantam women's fiction titles coming in June. *New York Times* bestselling author Amanda Quick stuns the romance world with **AFFAIR**. Private investigator Charlotte Arkendale doesn't know what to make of Baxter St. Ives, her new man-of-affairs. He claims to be a respectable gentleman, but something in his eyes proclaims otherwise. Fellow *New York Times* bestselling author Nora Roberts delivers **SWEET REVENGE**, now available again in paperback. Just as Princess Adrianne is poised to taste the sweetness of her long-awaited vengeance, she finds herself up against two formidable men—one with the knowledge to take her freedom, the other with the power to take her life. In the tradition of PRINCE OF SHADOWS and PRINCE OF WOLVES, Susan Krinard returns with **TWICE A HERO**. Adventurer Mac Sinclair is fascinated by the exploits of her grandfather and his partner Liam O'Shea. When she becomes disoriented inside the ruins in the Mayan jungles, she bumps into Liam O'Shea himself . . . alive, well, and seductively real—in the year 1884! Historical romance favorite Adrienne deWolfe puts the finishing touch on her Texas trilogy with **TEXAS WILDCAT**, a story about a man and a woman who are on opposite sides of the fence. As Bailey McShane and Zach Rawlins struggle with the drought that's tearing the state apart, they slowly realize that being together is the thing that matters most.

Don't miss these extraordinary books
by your favorite Bantam authors!

On sale in April:

MISCHIEF
by Amanda Quick

ONCE A WARRIOR
by Karyn Monk

Now available in paperback

MISCHIEF

by *New York Times* bestselling author

Amanda Quick

*To help her foil a ruthless fortune hunter, Imogen
Waterstone needs a man.
Not just any man, but Matthias Marshall,
the intrepid explorer known as
"Cold-blooded Colchester."*

"You pass yourself off as a man of action, but
now it seems that you are not that sort of man at
all," Imogen told Matthias.

"I do not pass myself off as anything but what
I am, you exasperating little—"

"Apparently you write fiction rather than fact,
sir. Bad enough that I thought you to be a clever,
resourceful gentleman given to feats of daring. I
have also been laboring under the equally mistaken assumption that you are a man who would
put matters of honor ahead of petty consider-
ations of inconvenience."

"Are you calling my honor as well as my man-
hood into question?"

"Why shouldn't I? You are clearly indebted to

me, sir, yet you obviously wish to avoid making payment on that debt."

"I was indebted to your uncle, not to you."

"I have explained to you that I inherited the debt," she retorted.

Matthias took another gliding step into the grim chamber. "Miss Waterstone, you try my patience."

"I would not dream of doing so," she said, her voice dangerously sweet. "I have concluded that you will not do at all as an associate in my scheme. I hereby release you from your promise. Begone, sir."

"Bloody hell, woman. You are not going to get rid of me so easily." Matthias crossed the remaining distance between them with two long strides and clamped his hands around her shoulders.

Touching her was a mistake. Anger metamorphosed into desire in the wink of an eye.

For an instant he could not move. His insides seemed to have been seized by a powerful fist. Matthias tried to breathe, but Imogen's scent filled his head, clouding his brain. He looked down into the bottomless depths of her blue-green eyes and wondered if he would drown. He opened his mouth to conclude the argument with a suitably repressive remark, but the words died in his throat.

The outrage vanished from Imogen's gaze. It was replaced by sudden concern. "My lord? Is something wrong?"

"Yes." It was all he could do to get the word past his teeth.

"What is it?" She began to look alarmed. "Are you ill?"

"Quite possibly."

"Good heavens. I had not realized. That no doubt explains your odd behavior."

"No doubt."

"Would you care to lie down on the bed for a few minutes?"

"I do not think that would be a wise move at this juncture." She was so soft. He could feel the warmth of her skin through the sleeves of her prim, practical gown. He realized that he longed to discover if she made love with the same impassioned spirit she displayed in an argument. He forced himself to remove his hands from her shoulders. "We had best finish this discussion at some other time."

"Nonsense," she said bracingly. "I do not believe in putting matters off, my lord."

Matthias shut his eyes for the space of two or three seconds and took a deep breath. When he lifted his lashes he saw that Imogen was watching him with a fascinated expression. "Miss Waterstone," he began with grim determination. "I am trying to employ reason here."

"You're going to help me, aren't you?" She started to smile.

"I beg your pardon?"

"You've changed your mind, haven't you? Your sense of honor has won out." Her eyes glowed. "Thank you, my lord. I knew you would assist me in my plans." She gave him an approving little pat on the arm. "And you must not concern yourself with the other matter."

"What other matter?"

"Why, your lack of direct experience with bold feats and daring adventure. I quite understand. You need not be embarrassed by the fact that you are not a man of action, sir."

"Miss Waterstone—"

"Not everyone can be an intrepid sort, after all," she continued blithely. "You need have no fear. If anything dangerous occurs in the course of my scheme, I shall deal with it."

"The very thought of you taking charge of a dangerous situation is enough to freeze the marrow in my bones."

"Obviously you suffer from a certain weakness of the nerves. But we shall contrive to muddle through. Try not to succumb to the terrors of the imagination, my lord. I know you must be extremely anxious about what lies ahead, but I assure you, I will be at your side every step of the way."

"Will you, indeed?" He felt dazed.

"I shall protect you." Without any warning, Imogen put her arms around him and gave him what was no doubt meant to be a quick, reassuring hug.

The tattered leash Matthias was using to hold on to his self-control snapped. Before Imogen could pull away, he wrapped her close.

"Sir?" Her eyes widened with surprise.

"The only aspect of this situation that truly alarms me, Miss Waterstone," he said roughly, "is the question of who will protect me from you?"

Her stories are tender and sensual,
humorous and deeply involving. Now
Karyn Monk offers her most enthralling
romance ever . . . a tale of a shattered
hero fighting for redemption—and fighting
for love. . . .

ONCE A WARRIOR

Karyn Monk

"Karyn Monk . . . brings the romance of the
era to readers with her spellbinding storytelling
talents. This is a new author to watch."
—*Romantic Times*

*Ariella MacKendrick knew her people had only one
hope for survival: she must find the mighty warrior
known as the Black Wolf and bring him home to
defend her clan. But when Ariella finally tracks him
down, Malcolm MacFane is nothing like the hero she
dreamed he would be. The fearless laird who once led
a thousand men is a drunken shell of his former self,
scarred inside and out, with no army in sight. Yet
Ariella has no choice but to put her trust in MacFane.*

And soon something begins to stir in the fallen legend. A fire still rages in his warrior heart—a passion that could lead them into battle . . . a desire, barely leashed, that could brand a Highland beauty's soul.

"Turn onto your stomach, MacFane," she instructed quietly.

He did not argue but simply did as she told him. Ariella suspected the powder she had given him had taken effect.

Now that he was on his front, it was far easier for her to massage him. She focused on the valley of his back for a while, and when she was finished, she placed one of the warm swine bladders on it, so the muscles could absorb the heat. Then she moved up, gently kneading the solid layers of spasm on each side of his spine. Little by little the hardness beneath her fingers began to yield. Her touch grew firmer, delved deeper, encouraging the muscles to release their grip. When her hands began to ache, she retrieved the other swine bladder, which she had kept warm before the fire, and gently placed it on his upper back.

MacFane's eyes were closed and he was breathing deeply, his head resting against his arm. Wanting him to be as comfortable as possible, Ariella removed his boots, examining his injured leg as she did so. He had told her it was shattered when his horse collapsed on it. She ran her hands up the muscled calf, bent it slightly at the knee, then continued her journey along his thigh. The bone seemed straight enough, and from what she could tell he had not lost any length. But she knew a bad break could plague a person with pain for the rest of his life. The leg was stiff, so she rubbed some ointment into her palms and began to massage it. After watching him limp this past month, she wondered if there was anything that could be done to ease the ache and strengthen the muscles. Perhaps with exercise—

"I didn't fall."

She looked up at him, surprised that he was still awake. "Pardon?"

"I didn't fall," he repeated thickly. "Someone put a spur under my saddle."

"I know." She continued to massage his leg.

He nodded with satisfaction and closed his eyes again. "I'm not in the habit of falling off my goddamn horse." The words were slurred, but she could hear the anger in them.

She thought of him thundering into her camp wielding his sword in both hands. No, MacFane was not in the habit of falling off his horse. Someone was trying to drive him away. The arrow hadn't worked, so they put a spur under his saddle, knowing the fall would not only injure him physically but would humiliate him in front of the entire clan.

"I think it was Niall," he mumbled.

She paused. "Why do you say that?"

"He has never tried to hide his contempt for me." He lifted his lids and regarded her a moment, his blue eyes suddenly intense. "And I've seen the way he looks at you." His expression was dark, as if the matter angered him. Then he sighed and closed his eyes once more.

Ariella considered this. Niall had shared her loathing toward MacFane when he failed to answer her father's missive. She had even encouraged his fury when her clan was attacked and MacFane never came. But while she could understand his expressing his contempt, could Niall actually be trying to drive him away? To do so would not be in the best interest of the clan. Was it possible his rage was that great?

Deeply disturbed by the possibility, she removed the cooling swine bladders from MacFane's back. He shifted onto his side, his head still resting on the hard pillow of his arm, his dark brown hair spilling loosely over his massive shoulder. Deciding she would bind his ribs with the linen strips tomorrow, she drew a blanket over him, then stayed there a moment, studying him.

He exuded an extraordinary aura of power and vulnerability as he lay there, injured and drugged, yet somehow still formidable. How cruelly ironic, that after fighting so many battles as the great Black Wolf, his greatest enemy now was his own body. Perhaps she had asked too much of him by bringing him here to train her people. From early morning to late evening he labored, training, planning, overseeing the fortifications to the castle. His demanding days would exhaust a man at the peak of his physical abilities, never mind one for whom it was an effort to cross a room or mount the stairs. And now someone was determined to force him from here, even if it meant injuring him in the process. It was wrong to expect he should remain under such circumstances, even if he had promised to remain until they found a new laird. She must send him away as soon as he was fit to ride, before he was even more injured than he had been today. In his current state he could do nothing more to help them. It was now up to her to find a warrior with an army who could wield the sword.

Yet as she stood beside him watching the even rise and fall of his chest, she could not help but wonder what would happen to MacFane when he left. He had no family or clan who would joyously celebrate his return. Instead he would go back to the dank, filthy hut he shared with Gavin, where his days would be nothing but long, empty hours filled with pain, drink, and bitterness. While this fact had never bothered her before, suddenly she found the idea abhorrent. However MacFane had failed his people, did he really deserve to be condemned to such a miserable existence?

His brow was creased, indicating he still struggled with his pain. He moaned slightly and buried his face in his arm, as if trying to escape his discomfort. A dark lock of hair slipped across the clenched line of his jaw. Without thinking, Ariella leaned over and gently brushed the hair off his face, her fingers grazing the sandy surface of his cheek. MacFane's hand instantly clamped

around her wrist, binding her to him with bruis-
ing force.

He opened his eyes and glared at her, his gaze
menacing as he fought to clear the mists of alco-
hol and herbs. When he realized who she was,
his grip eased, but he did not release her. Instead
he pulled her down, until she hovered barely a
breath away from him.

"I will not leave you, Ariella," he whispered
roughly, "until I know you are safe."

Ariella stared at him, her heart beating rapidly,
wondering how he could have known what she
was thinking. "You cannot stay, MacFane," she
countered. "Whoever wants you gone will not
stop until you are dead."

Malcolm released her wrist and waited for her
to move away from him. When she did not, he
hesitantly laid his fingers against her cheek. "I'm
already dead," he murmured, fascinated by the
softness of her skin. "I have been for a long
time."

They stayed like that a moment, staring at
each other. And then, overcome with weariness,
Malcolm sighed and drifted into sleep, his hand
still pressed against the silk of Ariella's cheek.

On sale in May:

AFFAIR
by Amanda Quick

TWICE A HERO
by Susan Krinard

TEXAS WILDCAT
by Adrienne deWolfe